"I have a contract, and I want my chickens!"

Melissa leaned over the desk, waving the contract in his face. "Mr. Winston, I have a college degree, I can read and write, and you can't tell me that there is anything that complicated about raising chickens."

"I am telling you just that." Dave looked into moss-green eyes. "This is business, and you simply don't qualify." His arm brushed hers, and he backed away as if he'd touched a hot wire.

Melissa raged with electricity. "Are you afraid I just might do a good job? You couldn't handle that could you?"

Dave wanted this woman to go away and stop disturbing his well-ordered life. "You want chickens?" he shouted. "I'll give you chickens. More chickens than you ever thought existed. I'll personally deliver them in the morning. In a few weeks, we'll see who's right."

Marcella Thompson worked with her sister under the name of Pamela Thompson to write a Harlequin Romance and an Intrigue, before deciding she needed to write some romance novels on her own. Her husband, retired from the federal government, runs a commercial blueberry farm in Arkansas, and during harvest, Marcella sets her writing aside and pitches in. Through her books, she likes to share with her readers the many wonderful, fascinating characters she's met in rural America.

Breaking Free
Marcella Thompson

Harlequin Books

TORONTO • NEW YORK • LONDON
AMSTERDAM • PARIS • SYDNEY • HAMBURG
STOCKHOLM • ATHENS • TOKYO • MILAN

ISBN 0-373-02802-4

Harlequin Romance first edition November 1986

CHAPTER ONE

DAVE WINSTON LOUNGED against the old oak tree in a pose as old as the practice of farming. The rough bark pressed against his back muscles, and one leg was bent sharply at the knee to allow the sole of a work boot a firm grip on the tree. Arms folded over his khaki-covered chest, he looked like all the other men leaning against various and sundry stationary objects as they watched the auction crowd. His Coors cap was pulled low, shading the pale-blue eyes against the brightness of the June day.

No one would suspect that Dave was the owner of a multimillion-dollar corporation, and that was the way he liked it. That was why he and everyone in the company from vice presidents to truck drivers wore the same khaki work suits. Dave Winston enjoyed anonymity.

The tree felt good against his back, and he moved from time to time, letting the rough bark soothe the strong muscles, which were knotted with tension all too often these days.

As he watched the crowd milling about, some examining items to be sold, others gathered in small knots visiting, he was glad he had come. He and his father had loved auctions, and every Saturday during the summer they had traveled to a different part of the county, but that had been many years ago. Today he found himself enjoying the show just as he once had. Not really sure why he'd decided to come, he rationalized that as president and sole owner of the neighboring Clear Creek Farms, he needed to know who would be buying this farm. When it came time to auction the real estate he'd find out.

But in fact, it was a warm June morning, and he felt a need to climb out of his role as executive and go back to his roots. A farm auction fit that bill just fine. Only the khaki trousers and shirt with the company logo told of his tie to the company. He nodded occasionally to farmers he knew, but mostly he just leaned against the tree and enjoyed the scene before him.

Dave watched the auctioneer work the crowd. The white pickup truck bore the legend, Col. Jake Henson, AMERICA'S GREATEST AUCTIONEER. Dave grinned at the logo and looked at the man standing on the bed of the truck, high enough above them to catch the slightest movement. Colonel Henson was probably in his fifties, gray hair showing under a bright yellow straw Stetson. A Western-style shirt and bright-blue jeans topped the expensive leather boots. He wore smoky-gray glasses, and a huge buckle, sporting the silver head of some fiery steed, peeked out under a belly that had known too much good Southern cooking and cold beer on hot summer days. But he was a master of his trade. He held the tinny public-address system mike close to his mouth and the gravelly voice exhorted the crowd to ever higher bids. His assistants stood on boxes at the edge of the crowd, scanning for any movement that might be construed as a bid, yelling "Yo" if they spotted a signal.

Shifting from one leg to another, Dave watched the crowd. A number of obvious tourists and outsiders scurried around, frantically bidding on things he knew would go in the trash heap when they got home. Farmers lounged about, chuckling over the bidding, waiting for a certain tool or item to come on the block. It wasn't that they needed it; it seemed more like it was something to remember their old neighbor by.

A certain magic envelops auctions, and this auction was no exception. The magic hooked people and they bought things, things they would never have considered buying anywhere else. Alicia had hated auctions. Dave put Alicia out of his mind, turning again to thoughts of his father. He remembered some of the things his father had dragged home from auctions, not because he needed them or even wanted them, but because they'd seemed such a bargain at the time, and because he'd got caught up in the magic. Dave smiled, wondering whatever had become of the old cast-iron turn-of-the-century lamp post he and Dad had hauled home one crisp fall day. He saw his mother's expression as clearly as if it had been yesterday.

An older man in overalls and a worn straw hat sidled up to Dave and tucked his huge callused hands under the bib of the overalls. "Haven't seen you around these parts lately, Davey. Buyin' or sellin'?"

Dave made no move to shake hands. That wasn't the way things were done. He gave the man a sidelong grin. "Neither, Homer. Just looking. You buying?"

"Nope. Just lookin'."

The men stood in silence for some time, watching the crowd. Homer Bates owned an adjoining farm and raised chickens for Dave's company, in fact had been one of Dave's growers for many years. "Anybody in the neighborhood interested in the place?"

Homer shook his head. "None I've heard. We're all gettin' too old to take care of what we got, let alone take on something new. You heard anything?"

"Nope." Dave was amazed at how easily he could slide back into the monosyllabic conversation he'd grown up with as a child. Farm people didn't waste words, yet nobody ever doubted what they were talking about. "How's Gertie?" Gertie and Homer had been married for as long as Dave could remember.

"Mean as ever." But the smile on the older man's face belied the words. The two lapsed into a comfortable silence.

Under the shade of the cap, Dave's eyes continued their perusal of the crowd, pausing to rest on a young woman wearing an Ocean Pacific sun visor. She reached up to push back the visor, and the auctioneer yelled, "Sold," pointing to her and bringing a smile to Dave's craggy face. The smile threatened to erupt into laughter as he watched her expression when she realized the item now belonged to her. Homer chuckled. "That little gal's gonna walk away with this farm if she ain't careful. That Jake knows a live one when he sees one."

Dave's eyes narrowed as he looked more closely at the trim figure encased in fashionably coordinated pale-green slacks and shirt. As she turned toward him, he glimpsed her face, somewhat ordinary at first sight. Then the long auburn hair caught the sunlight, causing it to shimmer, and although the visor shaded her eyes, he knew in an instant that they would be moss-green. He caught his breath as his gaze wandered over the small figure, sensing something, but unable to pinpoint it. Forcing himself to relax again, he decided she must remind him of Alicia. Angered by another unwanted thought of his ex-wife, and angrier still because he always seemed to be attracted to that type, he shifted once more against the tree and made himself think again of his reasons for being at the auction.

The farm up for sale had two modern poultry houses over the hill behind the house. The owner, an old man who had died recently, had raised chickens under contract to Dave's firm since before Dave could remember. The firm furnished the feed and the chickens and the farmer took care of them, providing the chicken houses and utilities. It was a good setup, close to town and easy to service. The company was scheduled to put thirty thousand baby chicks here Tuesday, and Dave hoped the farm would be sold to an experienced grower who could be ready by then.

Dave turned to Homer. "What's the mortgage on the farm, do you know?"

Homer shrugged. "Fifty thousand give or take."

Dave nodded and rubbed his back against the tree. "If the equity doesn't go too high on the block this morning, a good grower could make a nice living on the farm." And the firm would make money too, he thought. He assumed the bank would honor the existing mortgage. "I guess they're just selling the equity this morning?" The old man nodded.

His attention once again was drawn as if by a magnet to the auburn-haired girl-woman hurrying toward a compact car with the result of her ill-advised touch of the cap. Once there she began to talk and gesture to a man who, from the carefully styled brown hair to the expensive leather loafers, looked as if he belonged on the golf course rather than here. His stance was rigid and unyielding, and an unbidden thought popped into Dave's mind. *She doesn't belong with him.*

Putting that thought aside, he wondered idly what the relationship might be. Wife, perhaps? They appeared to be arguing, and even from a distance Dave sensed that the man overwhelmed her. For some strange reason, this angered him. He watched her turn and walk back to the auction, head down, step a little heavier. He thought she needed someone to protect her.

Laughing at his own seriousness, he began to wonder what she was doing in Viney Grove, Arkansas, and why she seemed to stand out in the crowd. There were plenty of other tourist types there. He let his eyes wander, but they seemed to keep tracking back to her, and finally he let his gaze linger. She wasn't that much different from a lot of other young women, yet . . . He swung his glance to the man by the car, then back to the woman, and his curiosity grew. Dave decided the warm June morning must be getting to him and headed for the refreshments. Better yet, he wouldn't hang around for the auctioning of the real estate. He started toward his truck, wondering why he'd noticed the auburn-haired woman in the first place.

MELISSA TALBOT was having fun. In her twenty-fifth year of life she had suddenly discovered a number of things heretofore unknown to her—all in one weekend—and all fun. She had the whole summer off, and she'd discovered camping in the Ozarks, much to the dismay of Henry, her husband-to-be. More importantly, she had discovered farm auctions, and she delighted in the discovery. She was having the time of her life.

Henry sulked by the car, anxious for her to tire of the adventure so that they could return to the city and civilization. Henry was definitely not having fun. But for Melissa, this excitement far exceeded anything she could have thought of to do in Tulsa. She already counted among her possessions an old maple chair she could refinish, a grease gun, an elderly almost-brass lamp, and a gallon jug labeled Cattle Dip. She wasn't really unhappy about the grease gun and the cattle dip;

it was more that she had no idea how she'd ended up with them. She was sure she'd bid on a cast-iron skillet and an antique iron.

But, she reflected happily, it seemed only a matter of getting the hang of what the auctioneer was saying. This was her first experience with auctions, and she felt she was catching on rapidly—well, most of the time. She noticed several other women in the crowd who seemed to have the same problem, but the carnival atmosphere made it all worthwhile. Melissa also noticed smiles on the faces above the overalls every time she or one of her soul mates carried off something like that grease gun. She did, however, wonder how she would explain these particular items to Henry, or worse, to her mother. Oh well, she would worry about that later. After all, she was of age, and it was time her mother stopped trying to run her life. Melissa wasn't sure this was possible, but it sounded good.

On her last trip to the car, she noticed that Henry was showing definite signs of unrest. He grew more flushed and sulky with each trip she made. She thought the cattle dip was the real culprit. Melissa realized she was living dangerously. Normally she never did anything to incur Henry's disfavor, but the excitement of the auction had temporarily freed her of her usual deference.

She looked at her latest purchase, an unidentifiable ceramic object with an electrical cord hanging from it, and cringed. A gray-haired woman standing beside her smiled first at her, then at the object. Whatever it was, all Melissa remembered about buying it was that she had pushed her visor back in order to see better. The auctioneer had yelled "Sold" and pointed to her.

The gray-haired woman gestured at the object. "I remember when Pearl got that. Her boy sent it to her from somewhere overseas." The woman looked at Melissa and continued, "He was in the navy. It always sat right on top of the TV." She saw Melissa stare at the garish object and turn it over in her hands. "It's a TV lamp. You put a bulb in it. Pearl always kept plastic flowers in it. She was afraid a bulb would start a fire. I never knew why she thought that."

Melissa examined the object again. "Oh."

"You're not from around here, are you?"

Melissa smiled, noting the statement held no malice. It was just an observation. "I'm from Tulsa. I've never been to an auction before." From her smile, Melissa sensed the other woman had already figured that out. "Are you from around here?"

The woman nodded. "Next farm over." Then she frowned. "You don't know how much I hate to see this place sell today. Pearl was just about the best neighbor anybody could ever have." She shook her head vigorously. "I do hate to see her leave. I sure hope whoever buys it will be a good neighbor."

Melissa stared at her. "You mean they're selling the house, too?"

The woman nodded. "Won't go for much. Nobody wants an old house anymore. And nobody wants to be out in the country. They all want them fancy houses in town, seems like." She chewed her bottom lip. "Sure would be nice to have some young folks around here. Kinda' keeps a body young themselves."

Melissa smiled at the wistful voice and headed for the car with her TV lamp.

When Henry caught sight of it, his rigidity increased by a factor of one hundred. "Melissa, you've had your fun. It's time to go."

Melissa never argued with Henry, but now she felt a seed of rebellion drop and take root. After all, she suffered through one weekend a month at Henry's seminars on soybean futures. He could at least let her stay through the auction. But it would never occur to Melissa simply to tell him she planned to stay. Her mother had seen to that. So she said, "Henry, I just heard some ladies talking. They're going to auction off the real estate at noon, and they say it'll go real cheap." She looked toward the house. "It would be perfect for weekends."

Henry turned a disdainful eye toward the modest little frame house. "Really, Melissa, what would we do with a shack in the middle of nowhere?"

Melissa looked at it once again with her long-repressed artist's eye. The simple gingerbread eaves showed bits of paint flaking, and the house perched on the edge of a long-abandoned millpond. Lilac bushes crowded the front porch, and the yellowing tops of jonquils told of last month's color. The whole scene seemed straight from a Currier and Ives calendar. Melissa thought it a lovely place and saw herself sitting beside the pond painting in the late afternoons. She gave a wistful sigh. The place stirred something deep inside her, unidentifiable, but deep and strong. She looked at Henry. She would never speak to Henry of stirrings—not of any kind.

She tried a different tack. "But Henry, it's lovely. After we're married, we could spend weekends and our vacations here. You could fish and I could paint, and..." She had to admit the house needed a little work, but the deep shaded porch with its old swing was irresistible.

Henry interrupted her thoughts. "After we're married, you'll be too busy entertaining and keeping house to paint, and I don't fish." He gave her a withering look. "People in our group vacation in Aspen or Florida, not the Ozarks. Now, are you ready to go?"

The closest to rebellion Melissa had ever come had been at age ten when she'd refused to take ballet lessons. Her mother had very carefully explained to her that nice girls didn't break their mother's hearts, and that had been that. But this morning she felt the seed planted earlier growing in the fresh air. "Henry, I've saved my money and you're always after me to invest it. Real estate is a good investment." A sidelong glance at Henry threatened to wilt both her and the tiny rebel plant struggling toward the sun. "I've heard you say that a lot," she went on lamely. "I could rent it or just hold on to it and sell it later." She suddenly felt shocked and excited at her casual use of the pronoun *I*.

Henry widened his stance, a sure sign of entrenchment. "Melissa, when I speak of real estate as an investment, I refer to condominiums in Florida, not shacks in the Ozarks. Kindergarten teachers hardly earn enough money for those kinds of investments." Melissa looked at the ground and he seemed to soften slightly. "After we're married, we'll look into the possibility of a condo if you're still interested in real estate."

Melissa wandered back to the auction crowd, her step heavy, her excitement deflated. She was well aware Henry was implying that any interest in something as serious as real estate must be just a passing fancy. *Well, what could you expect from someone whose life revolves around soybeans in the abstract?* she thought. Henry would make the perfect husband. Everyone, including her mother, told her so. But Melissa wanted to do something on her own for a change. No one seemed to take her seriously. She supposed it was because she was basically good-natured, and people mistook her for a doormat. She guessed her petite build and little-girl look didn't help.

It occurred to her that all her life people had told her what to do, and she had done it. First her mother, now Henry. That something stirred in her again. For once, she would do what *she* wanted to do and worry about the consequences later.

She rejoined the crowd and the magic, Henry forgotten for the moment. The auctioneer hitched up the jeans that threatened to defy his belt and motioned for silence. "Now boys, I want you all to listen close. All of you know Clarence made a good livin' on this place, and I want to see some bids that do right by his widow." He began to chant as he talked. "What am I bid? Twenty thousand, gimme twenty, twenty, twenty." He shook his head and adjusted his Stetson. "Boys, look at that house. You know what it would cost to build one like it today. And this land'll grow hay taller than my head. Gimme ten, ten, ten!"

Melissa's eyes widened, registering her shock at the low price. Her left hand grasped her right, which was threatening to wave at the man wearing the Western hat who was holding the mike.

The crowd grew silent. Melissa only had five thousand dollars in savings, but she began to envision the bargain of the century and again clutched the hand that now seemed to have a life of its own. Finally someone bid two thousand dollars.

Colonel Henson wiped imaginary tears from his eyes. "This land's worth more than that. Now you boys are tryin' to steal this place." His eyes zeroed in on Melissa and stopped. "How about you, little lady? Think about spending your summers in that lovely farmhouse. Step out here and catch fresh fish for breakfast. Got two, gimme three, three, three!"

Without stopping to think, Melissa heard herself yell, "Three thousand!" She flinched as the first bidder raised it another thousand. Nothing existed for Melissa now except the auctioneer's voice, cajoling the crowd to bid. She heard him tell them they were stealing the farm, that they ought to be arrested for this kind of bidding. She saw her dream begin to slip away. With as much authority as she could muster, she let her quivering right hand have its way, followed by what she hoped was not a quivering voice. "Four thousand, three hundred seventy-five dollars!" She hoped the odd amount would discourage the other bidder. She held her breath until her lungs threatened to explode. Silence.

The auctioneer continued his tirade at the crowd, and Melissa continued to hold her breath. Finally, after much lamenting, the man shook his head, muttered something about robbery and announced to the crowd that the little lady in the red visor was now the proud owner. Melissa stretched to her full five feet two inches and studiously ignored the incredulous faces of some of the farmers close by. Her dream saved, she didn't care what anyone thought. For the first time in her life, she owned property. Not even Henry or her mother could argue with this bargain. She inwardly congratulated herself that her first venture into the world of finance had been so painless and easy. The tiny rebel plant deep within her spurted upward, showing its approval.

She hurried to the cashier, anxious to claim her house before facing Henry. The woman smiled, showing one gold tooth in a row of otherwise even white teeth. Melissa felt as if they were old friends by now. The woman informed Melissa that she must leave a check with her for the amount bid, which would then be conveyed to the Farmers and Merchants Bank in Viney Grove first thing Monday morning. Melissa should report to said bank at the same time where the real estate papers and poultry contract would await her signing. The bank would take care of the closing.

Melissa brightened even more at the mention of a poultry contract. "You mean chickens come with the house?" Fond childhood memories of her grandmother, fat white hens and little bits of yellow fluff floated before her eyes.

The woman looked at her for a long moment, her tongue stroking the edge of the gold tooth. Then she grinned, as if at some private thought. "Yes, honey, chickens definitely come with the place."

Melissa wondered at the look, but passed it off, ignoring the frantic whispering at the cashier's table as she walked away. She must tell Henry. Henry would definitely not be happy. Melissa doubted that Henry knew the first thing about chickens, but somehow she knew he would hate them.

CHAPTER TWO

MELISSA FIDGETED in the stiff vinyl booth of the Baker Café, nervously watching the bank across the street and awaiting its nine o'clock opening. She felt excitement mingled with fear of the unknown. The weekend had seemed to race downhill after the auction, hardly what she'd expected during the planning of it. Henry had been furious that she'd bought a piece of property, and even more furious that she'd done it in spite of his warnings.

Melissa sensed that the combination of her showing rebellious tendencies coupled with a weekend of camping simply proved too much for Henry's sense of order. He had returned to his Tulsa office and his soybean futures late Sunday, reminding Melissa in a rather patronizing tone that he understood some women felt a bit adventuresome before they settled down to the duties of marriage. Furthermore, he deemed himself modern and understanding. She read between the lines the unspoken end to his statement: "as long as you don't get carried away."

It was a funny thing about Henry. Always before he'd seemed protective and solely interested in taking care of her. And it had been nice. Only this weekend, with Henry out of his element so to speak, had she seen some things that sounded an alarm inside her head.

But Monday was another beautiful day, and Melissa looked forward to a whole week by herself. She'd told Henry she would continue her camping expedition and get the little house ready for his inspection by the next weekend. Henry had been less than happy about leaving her alone in the wilderness, but had finally agreed. She looked at the clock again. Five more minutes.

Melissa realized she'd never spent a whole week by herself. She'd lived at home, then with roommates. Next would be Henry. She shivered at the prospect of the coming week, alone and the owner of a house. When she noticed through the windows of the café a person standing inside the bank, she quickly paid for her coffee and rushed across the quiet street, determined to be the first customer in the door.

After Melissa explained her purpose to the teller, the woman referred her to a Mr. Felker at the rear. She decided that the bank had probably not changed in years, and as she approached Mr. Felker, she decided he hadn't, either. He was an elderly man, probably in his late sixties, with thinning hair and wire-rimmed glasses. He looked just the way Melissa thought a banker should.

He glanced up as she approached. "Mr. Felker, I'm Melissa Talbut," she said in her brightest, most confident voice. "I'm supposed to sign some papers this morning."

Mr. Felker smiled, immediately, looking like everyone's grandfather. "Oh yes, you bought the Beadle place."

Melissa swelled with pride at the words. Yes, she'd bought a place and was handling it rather well, she thought.

Mr. Felker stood and waved her toward a chair. "If you'll just have a seat, I'll get the necessary papers."

Melissa sat straight in the old oak chair, tapping her foot and gazing around the bank's interior, really seeing it for the first time. The marble counters glowed with years of use and polishing, as did the marble floor. The tellers' cages were of polished wood, dark with age, and brass that had dulled to a soft patina. The vault behind Mr. Felker's desk looked like something from an old Western movie. It was quite unlike the modern gleaming banks she saw at home, and looked for all the world as if Jesse James might break down the doors at any minute and demand their money. Melissa liked it very much.

Mr. Felker returned with a handful of papers. His smile was benevolent. "Now, Miss Talbut, we have the mortgage papers and the poultry contract ready for you to sign, then we'll record them at the courthouse."

Melissa felt an uneasy sensation stir at the back of her neck. "Uh, Mr. Felker, are you sure you have the right papers? I paid for the place the day of the auction. Saturday. The woman said the check would be here this morning.''

Mr. Felker frowned and cleared his throat. Melissa knew from the look that Mr. Felker never had the wrong papers. "Miss Talbut, I assure you I have the correct papers. Now about the mortgage."

Melissa's voice squeaked. "Mortgage?"

Mr. Felker's smile told Melissa he'd never doubted the papers. "Yes, if you'd just sign here." He pushed papers toward her. "The balance of the mortgage is fifty-one thousand, four hundred twenty-eight dollars and seventy-eight cents. The first payment is due in September of this year and will be, uh, twenty-seven hundred and eighty-five dollars. The payments are currently set up on a semiannual basis, but of course we can adjust them to meet your needs." He stopped his monologue and stared at her.

Melissa muttered something like "How about never," and thought she must be drowning. She'd always heard that when you were drowning, your whole life passed in front of you. Well, here she sat in a quaint little bank in Viney Grove, Arkansas, listening to a quaint little banker tell her of disaster and ruination, and her life was indeed passing before her eyes. She must therefore be drowning.

"Miss Talbut, are you quite all right?" No reply. "You're not going to faint or anything, are you?"

Faint? She would much prefer to die. What would Henry say? Oh God, what would her mother say? One lousy little harmless bit of independence, and she ended up on the road to destruction. The rebel plant deep within her, which had flourished for two days, gave a gasp, then turned up its toes and died—right there in the Viney Grove bank. She managed to push her imminent destruction aside long enough to ask the burning question, her voice squeaking and shaky. "Why didn't I know about a mortgage?"

Mr. Felker flashed his now-familiar smile, seemingly happy the conversation was turning to something he liked to talk about, probably still happier that she showed no further signs of fainting. "Well, one should check into these things before doing anything drastic, like bidding. What your forty-seven hundred and some odd dollars bought was the equity on the place; that is, you bought the right to assume the mortgage." He clucked and waggled a finger at her. "It's quite standard procedure these days. Really, young lady, you should be more careful in the future, or have someone who understands these things check for you." The finger continued to waggle.

Melissa groaned at the mention of the future, as if there would be a future. Mother and Henry would love Mr. Felker. She marshaled her thoughts. "But I didn't know. No one said anything about a mortgage. Can't I get out of it?"

The finger waggled with new energy. "Young lady, ignorance is no excuse in the sight of the law, and you signed a legal document Saturday. You are liable for this mortgage." Seeming to fear she might faint at this bit of news, he relented slightly. "My advice is to put the place on the market as soon as possible and hope it sells before the payment is due." He tapped the desk with long fingers. "Although that is rather unlikely. Of course you could exercise the option on the poultry contract and raise chickens until the place sells. That would bring in enough to make the payment." He looked at the coordinated sportswear. "But then you probably don't want to raise chickens."

Melissa didn't see chickens. She saw a lifeline sailing toward her. She was free for the summer. She could raise a few chickens, make the payment, sell the place, and no one would ever have to know. She couldn't quite imagine making that size payment with a few chickens, but how hard could it be? "I'll raise chickens, Mr. Felker. Anything to save the money I've invested."

Mr. Felker smiled and began sorting through the papers. Melissa sensed he was pleased that she would soon be someone else's problem. "Well then, if you'll just sign here, here and here, we will take care of the rest of the matter."

Melissa signed everything, anxious to leave before the banker thought of any more disastrous details. "What do I do now? About the chickens, I mean."

"Just go over to Clear Creek Farms on Old Creek Road. Someone will help you." Melissa saw clearly that he doubted that last statement. "Just show them the contract. It goes with the farm."

Melissa forced shaky legs to carry her to the car, where she slumped in the seat. She experienced serious doubts about raising chickens, but was there an alternative? She must devise a plan, something that would prevent her from returning home in disgrace. More to the point, a plan that would stop Henry and her mother from ever finding out about this mess she'd managed to get herself into. She raised her head. She would grow chickens, and she would figure out some way to keep that information from Henry and her mother. After all, she'd got into this and she would jolly well get out of it. She was a grown woman and capable of handling the situation.

She glanced at the directions carefully drawn by Mr. Felker and turned her car toward Old Creek Road, suddenly finding herself driving up a paved road through manicured grounds. Ahead a buff brick building sprawled over a large area, and she found herself staring at a giant white chicken perched on the roof. She couldn't imagine what it was made of, but it was certainly impressive. To her right, large silos rose many stories high. Looking at the building, she realized that this was a big business, and involved more than a few chickens. Doubts assailed her once more.

She sighed, girding herself to go into the building. She'd made her plans, and now she must stick to them. She would worry later about how to handle Henry.

She walked through the door marked Business Office with a little more spring to her step. After all, what could be so hard about raising a few chickens? She handed the contract to a receptionist, asking to see someone in charge. Melissa noticed a twitch at the corner of the young woman's mouth as she buzzed a number on the intercom system. She also heard a not too friendly voice come back with a not too friendly "Yes."

"The new owner of the Beadle place is here, Dave."

"Send him in." The voice sounded deep and Melissa wondered what the man would look like.

"Yes sir, but it's a her."

Melissa fancied she heard an oath before the connection broke. The woman directed her to the first office down the hall. She knocked on the door and a booming voice yelled, "Come." Taking a deep breath and clutching her contract to her bosom, she opened the door and walked in, hoping she exuded a confidence she certainly didn't feel.

The man behind the desk stared at her as if she were a ghost. "I'm Melissa Talbut, Mr....uh..." She stared into the bluest eyes she'd ever seen. Words failed her.

The man continued to stare at her, then wiped a hand across his eyes. "Oh God..." The blue eyes pierced her very soul. "Don't tell me. What a way to start the week."

Melissa wondered if the man was experiencing some kind of seizure or if he was talking to someone else. She couldn't imagine why he would be saying such things to her. She tore her eyes away from the piercing blue to glance over her shoulder. The hallway was empty. Looking back toward the desk, careful to avoid the man's eyes, she noticed a small metal nameplate on the desk that read Dave Winston. "Mr. Winston, I have a contract here, and I'd like to talk to you about it."

She advanced toward the desk, determined to hold to her plan in spite of this man. She noticed for the first time the dark-blond hair and tanned skin, which made the eyes look even bluer. The face was rough and lined, making Melissa think of the Marlboro Man. She felt very peculiar, but attributed it to the fact she hadn't eaten breakfast. Or maybe this was just how business dealings affected her. She inhaled deeply. "I want to raise chickens." She tried to cover the squeaking voice with a dazzling smile.

Dave Winston recovered somewhat from the shock of seeing before him the girl-woman from the auction. He wasn't about to let her know he'd seen her before. This damn woman had wandered through his thoughts since Saturday, and now she'd come waltzing into his office wanting to raise chickens. He'd considered her in a number of lights since Saturday, but being a chicken grower certainly had not been one of them.

"You didn't really buy that place." He rubbed his eyes again, hoping she would disappear. "Tell me you didn't buy it."

Melissa had no intention of telling this stranger with the eyes that made her feel funny anything about the mess she'd managed to make of things. She would act like anyone else who wanted to raise chickens. At least she *hoped* she would. "Well, actually I did." She tried to avoid his eyes, but they drew her like a magnet. "I'm going to sell it later, but in the meantime, I'd like to raise a few chickens." She knew that didn't make a whole lot of sense, even to her. "I think it would be good experience for me, don't you?" She was digging the hole deeper and deeper. "You see—"

The blue eyes flashed with anger. "Spare me the details." What the hell was he going to do with the thirty thousand chicks scheduled for that place tomorrow? It seemed obvious this female preppy was not the answer. "Lady, I'm afraid that's out of the question. What do you really do for a living?" Calmer now, he looked squarely into her eyes. He'd been right. Soft woods' moss flecked with sunshine stared back at him.

"I'm a kindergarten teacher, but I don't see what that has to do—"

"The answer is no. You have absolutely no experience, and we don't take on growers to raise. We can't possibly honor that contract, and I believe if you'll read the fine print, you'll see that we have the option of refusal." Dave wanted her out of his office. He didn't want to look into those moss-green eyes that reminded him of spring and the woods and...other things. He stood and walked around his desk. "I'm sorry. Now if there's nothing more..."

Dave watched in horror as the green eyes began to glisten. He knew she was going to cry, and he knew he couldn't stand it. He raised his eyes from the tears to the rich auburn hair, and that didn't help at all. Backing away, he put the desk between them again. He didn't really understand why this woman affected him so, and right now, he didn't want to understand it.

Melissa knew the sound of authority when she heard it. She'd had plenty of experience with authority. Dave Winston was definitely authority, and her reaction to him came almost automatically, the result of long years of conditioning. The man stood there, telling her she was finished, ruined, and she was prepared to accept it. She rose slowly, looked for one last time at the eyes that seemed to be the cause of her drowning feelings and walked toward the door. *Nice girls don't argue with authority.* The man turned his back and stared out the window.

The warm sunshine hit her face, and she blinked back the last of the tears. She supposed she might as well go home, confess everything and take her licks. She frowned at the thought. Henry and her mother would never let her out of their sight again. She sighed and started the car. All she wanted was to be independent for once in her life, prove to herself she could do it. Obviously she couldn't. She started out the long drive, then that something stirred again deep within her very being, struggling to get out. She listened. She slammed on the brakes and wheeled the little car around in the middle of the driveway. No, damn it, she would not go back yet, and she wouldn't let that underling decide her fate.

New and exciting thoughts raced through her mind. This was her big chance and she would see it through. She would demand to see the owner of the company, and she would demand her chickens. After all, she held in her hands a contract.

She marched back into the building, not even stopping at the front desk. Her head held high, she marched unannounced into Dave Winston's office. "Mr. Winston, I'd like to see the owner of this place. I have a contract and I want my chickens." An energy previously unknown to her surged through her body.

Dave Winston opened his mouth, but found that no words came. Those wonderful green eyes flashed at him and the effect was devastating. Perhaps there was more to this woman than met the eye. But, while his curiosity at the sudden change in her behavior ran rampant, he also recognized danger when he saw it. This woman smacked of Danger with a capital *D*. For some reason he didn't want her to know he owned the company, and while this would have put an end to the discussion immediately, he chose not to tell her. "I'm sorry. I'm in charge of contracts, and my decision stands."

Melissa leaned over the desk, waving the contract in his face. She could smell him that close, after-shave mingled with...all that came to mind was...male. "I'll take you to court." Melissa heard the words and wondered where they'd come from—surely not from her mouth.

Dave's eyes were inches from the soft curves straining at the thin cotton shirt, and he clenched his hands around a paperweight to steady them. He felt the hairs prickle on the back of his neck. "No. And that's final." He flung down the paperweight, standing up with enough force to knock over his chair, and turned toward the window. He breathed deeply.

Melissa felt a moment of dismay, then the energy began to course. She would not be put off this easily, knowing she'd never have the courage to go through this again. She normally didn't argue with anyone, but something about this man... Well, she wouldn't back down. She pursued him to the window, standing inches from him, sensing his discomfort. "Mr. Winston, I have a college degree, I can read and write, and you can't stand there and tell me there is anything that complicated about raising chickens."

He turned on her, unaware she stood so close, and his arm brushed hers. He backed away as if he'd touched a hot wire. He saw her expression and knew the jolt had hit her too. "I am telling you just that. This is agribusiness." He heard his voice rise. "This isn't your grandmother's chicken coop we're talking about. And you just don't qualify."

Melissa was raging with the electricity of his touch, but had no idea of the source. All she knew was that something inspired further argument. "Are you afraid I might just do a good job? You couldn't handle that, could you?" Suddenly this man and his chickens had become the most important thing in Melissa's life.

Dave wanted this woman to go away and stop disturbing his well-ordered life. He had to get her out of his office and out of his life before he did something really stupid. He heard the words, but didn't believe he'd said them. "All right, lady. You want chickens? I'll give you chickens. More chickens than you ever thought existed. I'll personally deliver them in the morning, and in a few weeks, we'll just see who's right." He brushed past her again and stalked toward the bookcase on the far side of the office. "In the meantime, you'd better bone up on the subject."

He began pulling heavy books off the shelves, striding to her and dumping them in her arms until her eyes barely peeked over the top. Dave's anger at his own behavior far outweighed his anger at this woman. He couldn't believe it. Dave Winston, cool young executive, throwing a tantrum, acting like a teenager.

Melissa staggered under the weight of the books, getting glimpses of titles such as *The Modern Poultryman* and *The Veterinarian's Guide to Poultry Disease*. But mostly, she felt the brush of his hand each time he piled on another book. She trembled with the excitement of success, and something else she couldn't identify.

Dave piled on the last book and pushed her to the door, growling, "Read these. I'll be there at daylight."

Melissa staggered to the car and dumped the books onto the front seat. She felt exhausted, yet a calm unlike any she had ever known descended on her. Never in her whole life had she behaved as she had in there. She'd stood up for herself, and she'd won.

That must be the cause of her exhilaration. Blue eyes came to mind. Surely this feeling couldn't be related to Dave Winston. After all, she never reacted that way to Henry, and she was going to marry Henry. She started down the drive for the second time, smiling to herself and humming. She wouldn't lose her savings now, nor would she have to tell anyone about the mortgage, the chickens or anything else. She sped toward her new home with a smile on her face and the image of sky-blue eyes in her mind. She would prove to that man, to herself and to the whole world that Melissa Talbut could take charge of her life.

CHAPTER THREE

MELISSA STAGGERED to the bathroom at five o'clock the next morning, determined to be awake and at her best when Dave Winston and his precious chickens arrived. She had to admit she felt twinges of regret about her noble stance of the day before. Her determination to be awake proved a virtual impossibility. Melissa and mornings did not go well together, and as she stumbled to the kitchen to boil water for coffee, she noted with growing despair that it was still pitch dark outside.

She groaned, thinking people just shouldn't get out of bed when it was still dark. She'd stayed up late the night before, trying to wade through the mountain of books, then had slept on the floor. Not that there'd been any choice about that. By morning she was definitely feeling less than confident about raising chickens. It had all seemed so simple, but the books didn't seem to agree with that philosophy.

By five-thirty, she sat slumped in a lawn chair in the living room, the only sign of movement her right arm raising the coffee cup, then lowering it again. She stared out the window and watched the pale morning light turn to fiery red, amazed at the beauty. She had always thought sunrises basically disgusting because of the time of day they occurred, much preferring sunsets. But as she watched the morning arrive in such spectacular fashion, she decided she'd been missing something after all.

She'd downed sufficient coffee to get her body moving when the sound of vehicles in the drive forced her to stir. Opening the front door, she saw a large white bus followed by a white pickup truck, both bearing the now-familiar white chicken and the name of the company. They stopped and she watched Dave Winston get out of the truck. Her trepidation grew as he came toward her, and that strange feeling in her stomach began again as she watched the khaki-clad legs bring him closer. Shaking herself, she started down the steps. She noticed the crooked grin.

"Well, I'm surprised you're even out of bed."

Melissa was surprised too, but hoped the icy water splashed on her face an hour ago would carry her through. "I've been up for hours."

He paused before turning back to the truck, looking first at the designer jeans and bright-red T-shirt, then her sleepy eyes. "I'll just bet you have." He noted the fiery hair tied neatly in a bandanna. "I assume you want to go to the chicken house and watch this procedure."

Melissa felt uncomfortable at best in the company of this man, but she felt a moment of real panic when she realized she had no idea where the chicken houses were. She glanced around nonchalantly, assuming they must be over the hill behind the house. "I'll ride with you if that's all right."

Furious, she registered the laughter in his eyes, acknowledging that he knew exactly what had just passed through her mind. He gave her a mock bow and started toward the truck. As she passed the bus, she heard the muted peeps of what sounded like a very large number of baby chickens. She climbed into the truck and closed the door, shutting herself into a much too confined space with the smiling man. She could smell the fresh scent of soap and after-shave. She stayed as close to the door as possible and cranked the window down.

Dave Winston smiled to himself, sensing her discomfort. He would teach this little twerp to play farmer. And yet, as he glanced sideways at her, he felt that familiar stirring of curiosity—and something else that had hit him the day of the auction and every time afterward when he thought of her. He didn't like it one bit.

He had married a socialite whose only goal in life had been to get him out of the sticks so her opportunities to spend his money would be improved. She took her fair share when she left a few years later, but he'd found the cost cheap. And he was sure this one smacked of the same type—comfortable middle class, city bred, either looking for a husband, or would certainly grab one if given the chance. He'd been a fool to let her goad him into providing chickens. He glanced at the still figure beside him. Oh well, he'd turn her over to the regular field man and then he would not see her again. She'd probably go home, wherever that was, within the week. That would be best, because he smelled danger—and just a hint of jasmine.

Melissa remained silent as the truck climbed the hill behind her dream house. Just over the crest they pulled into full view of two structures that seemed to stretch forever, the morning sun glinting dully off metal roofs. A sound escaped Melissa as she sucked in air, her eyes growing wider as the buildings loomed larger. These certainly didn't look like her grandmother's chicken house. Then it hit her that these mammoth buildings were going to be full of chickens. The now-familiar drowning feeling washed over her. She idly wondered how many times a person could drown. Lord, how many chickens would it take to fill a building that big? Why hadn't she listened to Henry? She sighed. She'd made her bed, or dug her grave as the case might be, and she could not back down now.

She would not let this... this man know just how scared she felt at the prospect of all those chickens. In the past twenty-four hours, it had suddenly become very important to prove something to him... and to herself. She climbed out of the truck, trying to look calm and collected. She hoped her usual early morning zombielike behavior would be so interpreted.

Dave started toward the bus. "I don't suppose you know whether the water and electricity are working?"

"I'm sure they are. They are at the house. I went by the electric co-op yesterday, and they assured me there would be no interruption of service." She would not break down in front of him, but how on earth did she know whether there was electricity or water up here? She hadn't even known about the chicken houses until yesterday.

The two men in the bus piled out and began to carry big plastic flats into the first house. She heard the cheeping and suddenly she wanted to see the chicks. She hurried into the house after them and stopped dead in her tracks. The first sensation to assail her was an overpowering smell of ammonia, which threatened to shut down her lungs. A soft mocking voice spoke behind her. "You'll get used to the smell." She nodded, taking tiny breaths, not believing a word he said.

When her eyes stopped watering, she looked around the huge building. The sight both amazed and bewildered her. Looking down the seemingly endless length, she saw what looked like giant woks hanging upside down about two feet off the floor. Carefully placed in a circle under each wok sat squatty little domes of red plastic and flat pens. Running the length of the house was an assortment of pipes and hoses and she had no idea what else.

Her trance was broken by Dave. "I've told the men to put out feed, since you seem to have overlooked that item. You might want to watch so you'll know how to do it." She watched as the men pressed a button and feed poured out of a big metal pipe into a cart. They pushed the cart down the length of the house, stopping to fill each of the flat pans. Dave began to explain the various items. "I'll have them light the brooder stoves." Those must be the woks, she thought. He stooped beside a plastic dome, and she noted water in the bottom. "These are all automatic, but you have to clean them out every day or two. When the chicks are about ten days old, you pick up the pans and the small waterers and the chickens will use the automatic feeders and waterers."

Melissa was making frantic mental notes of everything he said. She watched in horror as the two men unceremoniously dumped the first several boxes of baby chicks out under the brooders. "Aren't they hurting them?"

"Melissa, we do this a lot, you know."

She hurried forward as chicks continued to spill out of the flats, piling up in big circles under the brooders. She wondered if there would be any hens to take care of them, but didn't want to ask. She had a sinking feeling that she was their mother for the duration. She gasped as she watched the little bits of yellow fluff scoot off in search of food. "Oh, they're beautiful!" She scooped up one and held it to her cheek, crooning and stroking the soft down.

Dave was taken aback by her reaction. He'd expected her to hate them. He tried to cover his reaction with anger. "This is not a pet shop, lady, this is a commercial poultry operation. We don't play with these birds, we raise them to process.''

Melissa refused the bait and smiled as one of the chicks left the group and ran cheeping to rest on her foot. She scooped it up, putting down the first. "I know, but how can anyone resist babies of any kind?" She picked up another chick. "They're so...fresh and smell so good." She rubbed the tiny chick against her nose.

Dave knew he had to get away from this woman. Although his company raised and processed hundreds of thousands of chickens each year, the hatching process and the tiny chicks still held a fascination for him that had never diminished. But he would never admit it and he was damned if this woman would ever see that side of him. He would be laughed out of his own business if anyone got a glimpse of him talking to a day-old chick.

He looked at Melissa, ready to throttle her for stirring up something in himself that he preferred to keep well hidden. But what he saw was a woman dressed more for a varsity football game than a chicken house, crooning to a bit of yellow fluff, which seemed to accent the rich auburn hair that had turned to flame in the morning sun. He saw an innocence in this girl-woman he'd thought long lost, and in that moment, Dave Winston knew he'd walked into a great deal of trouble. He knew that picture of creamy skin, fiery hair and a bit of yellow down would haunt him for days and weeks to come. And as he looked again, he knew he must get away from her or he would be lost in that picture. How could he have been so wrong? She should have turned up her nose at the first whiff of ammonia and told him to take back the chicks. But not only had she gotten through the ammonia, she loved the chicks.

He began pacing toward the door of the building, talking rapidly. "I hope you did your homework last night. You have to spend a lot of time with them the first week, making sure they eat and don't drown." He glanced up to see if she was paying any attention. Wide moss-green eyes added their part to the picture. He paced faster. "The side curtains are automatic. If it gets hot, turn down the brooders. There are thermometers scattered throughout the house. I'll have more feed sent out in a few days."

He glanced up. She was now on her knees in the middle of a circle of chicks, carefully showing each to the food pan and the waterer. Dave groaned aloud. She wasn't supposed to like any of this. His only consolation was his certain knowledge that she would tire of the chicks soon enough. That seemed to be the only thing of which he was certain. "Are you listening to me?"

She gave him a dazzling smile, which didn't help his humor at all. "I'll take care of them."

His eyes rolled back as she bent lower over the chicks. "I'll assign a field man to you. If you have any problems, call him."

Melissa frowned and somehow felt cheated. She sat back on her heels. "I thought you were going to help me."

"We have a regular field man for this operation."

"What's the matter? Afraid I just might be able to handle this and then you'd have to change your opinion?" Melissa was surprised at her assertiveness. She didn't want another field man. She wanted this one, wanted to see him again, to prove to him that she could handle this job. She stood up and walked toward him, sticking her face into what turned out to be his chest. "Well?" She tore her eyes away from those flashing blue eyes that threatened to suck her into them, only to find herself staring at coarse blond hairs curling out of the neck of his shirt.

At that moment Dave didn't know whether to swat her or run as fast as he could. He really wanted to run, but decided that was not the better part of valor for a man in his position. He brushed past her. "I only brought enough chicks to fill this house. I figured it would be all you could do to take care of these, let alone another houseful."

Melissa glanced around to see the men heading to the bus, then hurried to catch Dave. There didn't seem to be so many chicks actually. They certainly nowhere near filled up the house. "It doesn't look to me like you even filled up this one."

He turned to face her. "They do grow, you know. Don't worry. If they live, which I doubt, they'll fill the whole house in a few weeks."

Melissa felt a flash of anger and leaned closer to him, the curling chest hair suddenly inches from her face. She felt slightly light-headed, and quickly raised her head to stare into his eyes. "And why do you doubt they'll live?"

The eyes flashed. "Because you don't know what you're doing, that's why. You're playing at this, and when you get tired of it, you'll just walk away— abandon the chickens and go back to whatever it is you do when you're not playing farmer." He'd seen the type before. She might think the chicks were cute now, but he'd be proven right before it was over.

"I'll have you know I've never abandoned an animal in my life." Actually she'd never owned an animal. Her mother didn't approve of "lower creatures." But she knew she wouldn't abandon one if she had had one. "I'll take better care of these little things than anyone else, and that's a promise." Once again she found herself with the choice of glaring at the eyes or the curly hair, so she backed away.

"It can't be that hard or there wouldn't be that many people doing it." Melissa couldn't figure out for the life of her why she was saying all these things, but they just kept spilling out. Good girls didn't argue with people, particularly men, but this man stirred something in her she'd never experienced before. She looked up and saw the flashing blue eyes calm as something she couldn't identify, replaced the anger.

He took a deep breath. "I'll let you know about the field man." Dave stalked to his truck and drove off down the hill, cursing himself for getting involved in this mess.

He was gone in a cloud of dust, and Melissa was alone. She wandered back to the chicken house and surveyed the scene before her. Ten circles of fluffy down huddled under their respective brooders, the yellow broken only by the bright-red plastic water domes sticking up in their midst. The rest of the house, covered only with bright-yellow straw, was bare of chicks. It occurred to Melissa that it was a rather pleasing sight. She also realized the smell seemed much less noticeable now. She began shooing the tiny biddies to water stations and feed pans, plucking out a number that seemed intent on staying in the waterers. She picked them up if they seemed reluctant, crooning to them and dipping the tiny beaks into the food and water.

Time flew by, and when she looked at her watch, it read early afternoon. She straightened up, more or less, rubbing her back. Surveying her brood again, she was sure she'd bent over each chick at least once, but then how would she ever know? She began to suspect she would eat her words of the morning before much longer, yet deep down she felt something... satisfaction she guessed, about what she was doing. This was something she was doing all on her own, and she was enjoying it—so far.

She retreated to the farmhouse for a quick lunch and rest, pausing to look at the lovely millpond. Then she trudged back up the hill to tend to the now seemingly endless number of chicks. She gathered up those that seemed unable to cope with their healthier mates, putting them aside in a cardboard box.

When she finally noticed the sun begin to retreat, she took her box of biddies to the house, then went outside to flop beside the pond, feeling as though she would never move again. She was convinced they would find her body there in the grass when they came to bring more feed.

The shrill ringing of the telephone brought her to a very shaky upright position. The question that burned in her mind was not who was calling, but could she walk to the house? She knew her back would be bent forever. Picking up the phone, she heard her squeaky voice. "Hello?"

"Melissa, what took you so long to answer? It's Henry."

Melissa stifled a groan. What she needed right now was a hot bath and hot food, not Henry. "Oh, hi."

"Melissa, I have tickets for the ballet on Friday night. You need to be at my house no later than seven. We'll have a late dinner."

Melissa fell back on the floor. Oh, no, she thought, what am I going to tell him? "Yes. Well, actually, Henry, I don't think I can make it." She held the receiver away from her ear, waiting for the explosion. It didn't happen. That, she knew from experience, was a much worse sign. It boded ill for what was to come. The voice in her ear sounded icy, and Melissa visualized Henry swelling with anger. She thought suddenly of a toad and stifled a giggle.

"Melissa, did I understand you to say you can't make it? I can't imagine any possible reason that would justify your action, but I suggest you try to explain. They don't give away ballet tickets, you know."

Melissa's mind raced. Henry definitely did not need to know what she'd been doing all day, and would probably be doing for several weeks to come. "Well, the house isn't ready." It sounded lame even to her.

"I fail to see what the condition of that awful house has to do with anything."

She heard the increasing tightness of his voice. "I've got plumbers coming on Saturday, and I need to be here."

"Really, Melissa. That may be the wilderness, but you can't make me believe plumbers work on Saturday there any more than they do here." A long silence ensued. "Just what is going on, Melissa? Do I have to drive over on Saturday and see for myself, or are you coming here Friday?"

Panic swept Melissa. She would have to tell him the truth. She pushed herself to a sitting position. "Henry..." Well, a little bit of the truth. "You see, I came into a few chickens today. Baby ones." She took a deep breath and plunged ahead. "I just can't leave them right now." She tried to laugh, but squeaked instead. "They're too young to leave alone."

The roar deafened her and she fell flat on her back again. "Chickens? Chickens, Melissa? Really, I don't know what's come over you since you retired to the wilderness, but my patience is not endless. Furthermore, I do not appreciate playing second fiddle to a gaggle of chickens!''

The emphasis on the last word indicated clearly to Melissa that Henry equated taking care of chickens with nursing plague victims. ''Flock, Henry.'' Melissa thought a change of subject might be in order.

''Flock? What the hell are you talking about, Melissa?''

A curse from Henry was a sure sign he was losing control. ''A gaggle is geese, Henry. I think geese would be very nice for the pond, don't you?'' Silence. ''This is such a lovely place, Henry, and I hope to start painting the house this week.''

''Your mother is quite concerned about you, Melissa. She thinks you should come back here where you belong.''

''You've talked to Mother?'' Melissa sat up straight, ignoring her protesting back. This was serious. If her mother and Henry combined forces, she didn't stand a chance.

''Of course I've talked to your mother. She's hurt that you would buy that house without consulting her. We're both planning to come over in a week or two and try to talk some sense into you.''

Melissa quickly considered her options. She could kill herself, or possibly join the merchant marine. Either would be far preferable to Henry and her mother finding out about the mess she'd gotten herself into. And she knew that if they ever came to this place, they would find out. "You have to wait until I'm through painting. I want you to be surprised." She tried to sound sincere. "I'll let you know when it's finished."

"The condition that shack's in, painting could take forever."

If Henry only knew that that was exactly what she had in mind. "Oh, it shouldn't take too long."

"Yes. Well, I'll talk to you in a few days."

Melissa put down the phone and staggered to the kitchen. She had to keep up her strength, so she had to eat. Hearing soft cheeping, she turned on the light and bent down to peer under the towel into the box of chicks. The dozen biddies seemed a little stronger, blinking at her and the light. She touched each one, determined they would live and thrive.

She decided a peanut butter sandwich was all she could manage before a hot bath. She began peeling off her clothes as she ate. She was down to underwear when the phone rang again. Knowing it must be her mother, she determined to take the offensive, or at least try. "Mother, in spite of what Henry says, I'm just fine." Silence.

Then a soft voice. "Melissa, this is not your mother."

Melissa recognized Dave Winston's voice with a shock. She scrambled to cover herself with little success. "Mr. Winston?" Peanut butter smeared itself over the receiver as she tried to hold the sandwich and the phone in one hand and grab a towel with the other. It took a moment to realize that he couldn't really see her. The voice seemed to be right in the room.

"I forgot to tell you something today."

"What?" Had she already done something wrong in ignorance?

"Uh . . . about the feed." Dave suddenly realized he should have thought up a story before being stupid enough to call her. "They'll deliver it tomorrow."

"That's nice." Melissa seemed to be very warm all of a sudden, even though she didn't have her clothes on.

"How are the chicks?"

"Fine." Should she ask him about the ones at her feet?

The voice seemed to change from silky to gruff. "I just wanted to check. Good night."

"Good night."

Dave slammed a fist into the back of the chair. Why had he called her? He couldn't seem to get her out of his mind. He wondered if she'd been getting ready for bed. That thought caused a chain of images he quickly squelched. He got up and poured another drink, looking around the elegant house where he lived alone, wishing he were somewhere else.

Melissa stood clutching her towel, staring at the phone. Her actions seemed silly now. She reclaimed the remains of the sandwich and headed for the bathroom. She knew she had changed in the past few days. She didn't really understand all the changes, but she knew she would stay here long enough to raise the chickens. She would also show her mother and Henry, and most importantly herself, that she could do it. But it would not be easy. She wondered if she could really stand up to her mother. It was something she'd never even dreamed of.

As the face of Dave Winston floated across her mind's eye, it seemed important to prove something to him, too. This she didn't understand at all. He was only a field man, but Melissa wanted him to know she was a whole person, not the wimp he obviously thought her to be.

She returned to the kitchen to crumble up more oatmeal for the biddies, then headed back to the bathroom, determined to soak away her aches in a hot tub. She actually felt less tired now. She had a real purpose. Fifteen thousand babies needed her, were depending on her, and she would not let them down.

Lowering herself into the steaming water, she realized no one had ever really needed her or depended on her, except at work, and somehow that just wasn't the same. A warm, nice feeling enveloped her. Her thoughts strayed to those blond curly hairs peeking out of a khaki shirt, and it crossed her mind that she would like to touch them. She flushed, aware for some reason of her nakedness. She'd never had a thought like that in her whole life. As she settled back, warm feelings enveloped her once again. Thinking strange new things seemed kind of good, too.

CHAPTER FOUR

MELISSA OPENED one eye and groped for the alarm clock. Darkness surrounded her, but she knew it must be five-thirty. For a moment she considered the possibility that the clock had gone off early, but realized that was too much to hope for. Her next concern was whether or not she could get up off the floor. As she raised herself for the attempt, muscles screamed their refusal. She lay back down. If one had a bed, one could just roll out of it; but a sleeping bag on the floor was a wholly different matter. Perhaps she could roll over and get up on all fours she decided, and lay quietly for a moment before making the attempt. She thought farming was a lot of work. She'd never been quite this stiff and sore, and knew it was from the thousands of times she'd stooped over the little biddies the day before.

Finally she stood, somewhat unsteadily, rubbing her stiff, sore back. The sky showed no signs of daylight yet and Melissa didn't really want to be up, but at least now she knew the sunrise would be beautiful, and that helped. She might even learn to like mornings, though she rather doubted it.

Staggering to the kitchen for life-sustaining coffee, she stopped at the box of chicks. They showed little more enthusiasm for the morning than she did, fussing until she put the towel back in place. She really couldn't figure out why it was necessary to get up so early. Didn't late to bed, late to rise end up in the same number of hours as early to bed, early to rise? Perhaps love of mornings was genetic or something.

Melissa quickly consumed enough coffee to get herself moving, and by the time she started for the chicken house, the sun had set the eastern sky on fire. She stood watching, again struck by the beauty of the morning sky reflected in the millpond. Her fingers itched for paints and a pad. She stopped again halfway up the hill, the sky now glowing orange, and wondered if she could capture the sight in a painting. She doubted she was coordinated enough to paint at this time of day, but felt sure that one day she would try.

Quickly ascertaining that her chicks seemed to be doing well, she walked the length of the house. The fluffy bits of yellow down were huddled under the warm brooder stoves this morning, but she noticed some that didn't seem to look right. A few showed places where they'd been picked on by others, and several just looked droopy.

She gathered them into the box brought along just for that sort of thing and started back to the house. She hadn't the first idea what to do for them, but some instinct told her they would have a better chance at the house with a little more attention. She wondered about calling Dave Winston and asking him what to do.

At the thought of Dave Winston, she felt a hint of warmth start deep within her. She clutched the box of chicks tighter and wondered why she had all these strange feelings whenever she thought about him. They were even worse when she was close to him. Never having had feelings like that before, she wasn't sure she liked them. Well, actually, she liked them very much, but she was certain she really shouldn't. No...she wasn't certain.... It was all too complicated and confusing to think about so early in the morning.

In the kitchen, Melissa sorted all the chicks according to their apparent malady and stared in shock to see that boxes almost covered the kitchen floor. She would definitely have to call someone to look at the chicks. She would also have to get more boxes. Smiling at the busy chicks, she knew none would die because of negligence on her part. She decided to wait until eight o'clock to call. To kill time, she crumbled more oatmeal for the chicks and changed their water. Picking up one, she rubbed the downy creature against her cheek.

When her watch showed eight o'clock, she dialed the number, giving her name to the woman who answered. After she waited what seemed a long time, a deep voice answered. "Winston."

At the sound of his voice, Melissa suddenly felt nervous and butterflies busied themselves in her

stomach. "Uh, Mr. Winston, this is Melissa Talbut.
I'm the one..."

She could have sworn she heard a muffled oath. "I
know who you are, Melissa."

Melissa felt a slight tingle as the deep voice drawled
out her name, and the butterflies increased their ac-
tivity. "Well, I...I need some help."

There was a slight pause. "I'm sure you do." Another pause. "Could you be a little more specific as to
what kind of help you need?" The voice was silky, but
she heard the mocking tone. He was making fun of
her, and she didn't like it. After all, she had every right
to ask him for help with her chickens. She held a contract.

The irritation at his attitude cleared her mind. "Mr.
Winston..."

"Dave. Since we're practically going steady, call me
Dave."

"I beg your pardon?"

"Joke. Now, what can I do for you?"

"Well, I have several chicks who don't seem to be
doing so well, and I'd like you to come out and look
at them. I don't know what to do for them." The
pause seemed to go on forever. "Are you still there?"

The voice no longer mocked, but hinted at some
emotion she couldn't identify. "Yes. Listen, three
percent of those chicks will most likely die. That's just
the way it is. As long as you are within the acceptable
levels, don't worry." The voice sounded strained.

Anger flashed through Melissa. "Mr. Winston, that's really crass. As far as I'm concerned the death of even one of these chicks is not acceptable. Now are you going to come out and check them, or do I have to call a vet?" Melissa feared, even as she heard herself utter the words, that vets probably didn't see chickens.

The voice softened, and Melissa sensed he was smiling. "Melissa, local vets don't treat chickens. We handle all that internally." He cleared his throat. "And I don't mean to sound crass, but some of the chicks are weak and just don't make it. If there really is a problem, we'll handle it."

Melissa thought for a moment, not sure what to do now. He sounded almost willing to come. "Well, why don't you handle it then? I have a contract, and I need help." No response. He must be weakening. "If you won't help me, perhaps you could refer me to someone higher in the company." Again a long silence.

"Okay. I'll come out this afternoon and check, but I'm telling you right now, I won't do anything if everything looks acceptable."

"Fine. Then you just tell me what to do and *I'll* do it." Melissa was amazed at the fire this man seemed to provoke in her. Her cheeks burned. But she had no intention of seeing death as acceptable. It wasn't in her nature. She imagined more muffled oaths, then snatched the receiver away from her ear at the unmistakable sound of another one being slammed down at the other end. She sat staring at the phone.

It was easy enough for him to talk about acceptable mortality rates. After all, he wasn't sitting in his office surrounded by boxes of chicks that didn't look so good. What was she supposed to do with them? Just throw them out somewhere to die? Melissa shuddered at the thought.

She thought back to the scene when they had brought the chicks. Dave Winston had acted a little oddly then. He'd acted as if he were angry with her, and Melissa couldn't think of any possible reason for that. He was a strange man, she decided, as she started back to the chicken house. She might have to see his supervisor before this was over. At least the butterflies seemed to be quiet now. Probably she ought to eat breakfast in the mornings.

MELISSA WALKED through the chicken house every two hours, although Dave had said every three or four hours was enough. She liked to err on the safe side in all things. By the time she'd checked the chicks in a manner she thought acceptable, it was time to start all over again. Morning became noon. She trudged down to the house to eat, clutching the latest box of problem chicks to her bosom. By the time she'd got them all sorted, she realized she needed more boxes.

She decided to go into town while she ate. That way she wouldn't be away from the chicks so long. She stopped in front of the store to finish her sandwich, glancing at the bank across the street, wondering whom Mr. Felker had in his clutches that day. She stared down the nearly empty street, liking the quiet serenity of the town, so unlike the city. There was time to look and see in a place like this.

Shaking off her thoughts, she headed into the store. She got all the empty boxes they had, persuaded the clerk to empty a few more, then headed home, thinking she really liked the little town. Too bad she couldn't stay.

When she'd shuffled the chicks around to new boxes, she realized there were over a hundred of them. The boxes were beginning to spill over into the living room. Oh well, she didn't have any furniture anyway. She noticed with a smile that the ones she'd brought down the day before seemed much better. Perhaps they could be returned to the flock in a few days.

She started out the door and saw a gray-haired woman walking around the millpond toward her. She recognized her as the woman who'd talked to her at the auction. The woman smiled and wiped her hands on a calico apron before extending one to Melissa. "Hi there. I'm Gertie Bates, and I just wanted to welcome you to the neighborhood." She looked at Melissa's stained pants and frazzled appearance. "And to see how you're doin' with the chicks."

Melissa shook the woman's hand, grateful to see a friendly face. "Thanks, and I don't know how I'm doing. Oh, I'm Melissa Talbut." She noted the woman's smile. "Actually I don't know *what* I'm doing. Do you raise chickens?"

The woman nodded. "Close to twenty years now. And I'd be more than happy to help you any way I can. Are you havin' problems?"

Melissa heaved a great sigh of relief. "Oh, Mrs. Bates, you can't imagine how glad I am you're here. Could you come see the ones in the house?"

Gertie raised an eyebrow, then said, "Everybody calls me Gertie." She followed Melissa into the house.

Melissa saw a strange expression cross Gertie's face as she surveyed the many and varied boxes that lay scattered over the floor. She followed the trail into the kitchen, stooping occasionally to lift a cover and look at the inhabitants. "Uh…Melissa, what are you doin' with all these chicks here at the house?"

"They didn't seem to be doing too well with the others."

Gertie looked at her and shook her head. A slow smile crinkled the face. "That's just what I used to do. All the men laughed, said they were gonna die anyway, so I finally quit it." The smile broadened and the blue eyes twinkled. Gertie Bates was a tall woman, tall and thin. She stretched to her full height as if the scene somehow took a load off her shoulders. "Lord, this sure does bring back memories. Womenfolk hate to see any little thing die, but men just don't seem to feel that way. You're gonna lose some of the chicks, honey. Can't be helped. But it makes me proud to see you try."

Melissa felt defiance rise within her. "Some may die, but it won't be because I didn't try."

"You just keep fightin' for 'em, honey. Now I'm bakin' this afternoon and just thought you might like a nice loaf of bread for your supper."

They walked toward the door. "I'd love it."

"Fine. I'll bring one over a little later." She stopped and looked hard at Melissa. "I somehow don't think you're gonna like raisin' livestock the way they do it these days." Her eyes narrowed. "They say you get used to it, but don't believe it. I never have." Her eyes shifted toward the house. "Sure does seem empty without Pearl and her things here. Do you have any furniture?"

Melissa laughed, knowing Gertie had looked carefully at the two lawn chairs and sleeping bag in the living room. "I guess I do need a few pieces, don't I?"

"You're welcome to borrow anything that's in my attic. Probably furnish a whole house out of that attic." She started toward the road. "Don't get too attached to those little things. They'll come for 'em before you know it."

Melissa wondered at Gertie's remarks about raising livestock and getting attached to them. She hadn't thought about the chicks growing up and being taken off somewhere. She had a feeling Gertie was right about her not being cut out for this.

The afternoon passed all too quickly, and Melissa returned for a quick meal and to check the house brood. She found a loaf of homemade bread still warm from the oven, inside the door. Within minutes she sat munching the plain bread, savoring every bite.

She kicked off her shoes, propped up her tired feet, and relaxed for the first time that day. After two days with fifteen thousand chicks, she mulled over the idea that twenty-five five-year-olds were not so bad after all.

Hearing a truck in the drive, she hurried to the porch, brushing bread crumbs off her shirt. With a sinking feeling she saw that the truck belonged to Dave Winston, and that he was wearing the worst scowl she'd ever seen. She watched the long strides carry him toward the house, and stepped off the porch to meet him, anxiety knotting the bread in her stomach. The butterflies began to dance again. They danced faster as she watched his eyes wander slowly from her bare feet until they came to rest on her shirt. Self-consciously, she looked down at the dirt- and sweat-streaked shirt that had been so clean that morning. Mindful of stones, she gingerly picked her way across the yard.

Dave Winston's scowl deepened as she came down the steps. Her auburn hair looked tousled and dirt and sweat streaked her creamy complexion. He supposed she'd actually been to the chicken house. That was more than he'd expected.

Dave took a deep breath. He would check the chicks and get right out of there. He stopped halfway and turned back to the truck, knowing instinctively there was nothing wrong with the chicks. New growers tended to panic. He wanted to leave. "Get in and let's go." He noticed she still stood halfway across the yard, one bare white foot resting on top of the other. "Look, I'm busy. If you want me to check the chicks, let's go."

Melissa chewed her lower lip, the authoritative voice ringing the old bell of her conditioning. Do what the man says. Her voice squeaked. "Uh...they're in here." A hand waved toward the house.

Dave tried to control his surprise. She hardly looked the type to seduce a man, but then you never knew. Not that he was totally opposed to the idea. On the other hand, being invited in to look at sick chickens certainly was different and original. Well, he'd play her game. Why not? "In the house?"

"In the house."

Dave swaggered just a little as he walked up the steps. Then he heard the unmistakable sound of cheeping. She didn't want to seduce him; she'd filled the damn house with chicks. He stopped and stared at her. "In the house!" He brushed past her as she held the door.

Nothing could have prepared him for the sight that greeted him. Boxes. Every imaginable size and shape of box stretched from the living room into the kitchen, each covered with its own bit of towel or scrap of cloth. He listened to the scratchings and muted cheeps and knew all the boxes contained chicks. He passed a hand over his face. This must be a dream. He noticed, however, that the sounds did not go away. He kept a steady voice. "What's wrong with them?" He turned to look at Melissa.

Melissa had felt a prickle on her arm when Dave brushed against it, but she felt more comfortable now that she could talk about her little charges. At least he hadn't laughed. "I've got them all separated according to what seems to be wrong with them." She bent over and lifted the towel from a box bearing a Hunt's catsup logo.

She felt his eyes on her. "These seem to be hurt. I noticed spots of blood on them. The others picked on them. These," she said, moving to an Ivory Soap box, "are crippled." She continued to move through the maze of boxes. "These just seem a little droopy." She straightened to see him staring at her, a glazed look in his very blue eyes. As soon as her eyes met his, her skin began to feel uncomfortably warm and the butterflies danced with a vengeance. "What should I do with them?"

Silence. Melissa wondered if he was in the midst of another spell. "Mr. Winston, I said what should I do with them?" She saw his mouth open, but no words came. She picked her way through the boxes and tugged at his sleeve. Her hand rubbed against the tanned skin and she jerked it back. "Are you all right?"

Suddenly his eyes lost the glazed look and flashed at her. "Melissa, for God's sake, you don't bring sick chickens to the house. Some of them die, that's all."

She stared at him. He seemed to be mad at her again. Melissa decided he really must be subject to some kind of spells. One minute, his eyes were glazed over, the next, they flashed in anger. She watched his jaw quiver. "Well that's not good enough for me. I have no intention of letting them die if I can save them." She felt very warm.

Dave tried a more official tack. "You will lose around twenty or thirty a day for the first week. That's what we expect." He glanced at the boxes of chicks and turned his back on them.

Melissa considered him cruel and heartless. Gertie was right. "Why? Are you telling me they can't survive?" She waved a hand over the boxes.

"No. By bringing them in and giving them special attention, they will most likely survive. But that is seldom done."

Melissa couldn't imagine why her bringing the chicks to the house had upset him so. Even if he didn't want to help with them, it was no reason for him to be so testy. "Why isn't it done?" Melissa needed some fresh air. She couldn't seem to breathe.

"Because we run a business. This is not a baby-sitting service, it's big business." His voice boomed in the small room. "And I'm telling you that you'll lose about three percent of the birds."

Tears glistened in Melissa's eyes. Her voice quavered. "And I'm telling you, that's not acceptable to me. Now tell me what I need to do for these." She looked up at him through a mist of unwanted tears and saw him reach for her, then pull back. She sensed something different in him, saw it for a fleeting second in his eyes. But Melissa didn't want this man to comfort her. She wanted help.

He tipped up her chin with a gentle finger until the mossy eyes looked through their curtain of tears into his. "Melissa, why is this so important to you?"

Melissa looked into the blue eyes. She wanted more than anything to tell him that this summer and these chicks would determine whether she was a real whole person, or whether she was incapable of managing her own life and would have to let Henry take over from her mother. But she was afraid he would not understand. She didn't understand all of it. "Because..." She resorted to the old childhood answer until she could think of a better one.

His voice came back gentle but persuasive. "Because why?"

She flipped back her hair and tried to look defiant. "I always try to do a good job whatever I take on. Isn't that reason enough?" She felt very warm now, and the spot on her chin tingled where his finger had rested.

"No, but we'll leave it for now. Would you have dinner with me, Melissa?"

Melissa frowned, certain she'd heard what she wanted to hear, not what he'd actually said. "I beg your pardon?"

Dave saw her confusion as he looked into her wide eyes. "Dinner. You know, when people go out and eat together?"

"Well, I don't know. I mean, I don't think I should leave the babies for that long." She tried to back away, but her feet refused to move.

His voice seemed to caress her body. "Melissa, I own... I mean I know about chickens, and I think they'll be just fine. Anyway, I was thinking about tomorrow night."

"Well, if you think..."

Dave knew she would worry about them all evening. "Better yet, I'll bring a picnic, then we can both check on them. How's that?"

"I guess that would be okay." Melissa had to get out of these close quarters and breathe some fresh air. The smell of...man threatened to smother her. "I think I'd better go check the big house again." She didn't know what else to say. He wasn't angry now. He was ... Melissa wasn't sure what he was now, but he kept looking at her and shaking his head, as if he'd just been told something that didn't make sense. At any rate, she thought fresh air was definitely in order. She started for the door as Dave backed toward it in front of her. She couldn't imagine why he didn't turn around and go out the right way. He acted as if he was afraid to get too close to her. His jaw still twitched, but this time around a smile.

"I'll see you tomorrow, and don't worry about these guys." He waved at the boxes. "They seem to be in the best of hands."

Melissa walked to the porch with him and watched him stop and look at the millpond, then shake his head. For a minute, she thought he might jump in. The truck disappeared in a cloud of dust while Melissa watched, her fingers stroking the place on her chin where his finger had burned its print. She felt bemused and tingly all over, a feeling she'd heard of and read about, but never experienced. She realized in a flash that all these strange feelings and butterflies related to this man, and her wonder grew.

She'd certainly never felt tingly with Henry. Her eyes grew large and a hand flew to her mouth. Henry. She'd forgotten all about Henry. What would he think if he knew she was going to have dinner with another man? Henry would not approve. The long conditioning caused momentary fear to surface, but she willed it away. She started up the hill. "Frankly, my dear Henry, I don't give a damn what you think." The sound of her voice—and its message—shocked her. This wasn't the Melissa everyone knew. It worried her, but at the same time, she felt free, and she liked the feeling. Somehow, Henry and a chicken farm just didn't seem to be compatible worries.

Melissa sat on the porch, pondering the events of the last hour. The millpond lay like a mirror in the late afternoon sun. A calm seemed to settle over her. Time slipped away. Melissa finally shook herself back to reality when she heard the phone ringing. She thought seriously about not answering it, because it had to be Henry or her mother. Knowing that if her mother didn't get an answer she would probably call out the

National Guard, Melissa succumbed to the persistent ringing. "Hello?"

The voice boomed across the line. "Melissa, where have you been all day? I was about ready to call the authorities."

"I've been busy, Mother." Melissa leaned against the kitchen counter.

"Well, of course, I would have called last night, but I didn't know. I had a club meeting last night and that dreadful Agnes went on and on."

Melissa thought she'd missed something crucial. "Mother, what are you talking about?"

"The ballet, of course. Henry is very upset."

Of course, Henry. "Mother, I explained to Henry."

"Melissa, you just don't tell a man that chickens are more important than the ballet. That is what you told him, isn't it? It's very bad for his ego."

Melissa doubted that chickens or anything else could damage Henry's ego, but that wasn't the sort of thing to tell her mother. "Mother, I just can't leave right now. He ought to understand."

"Besides, they carry disease, don't they?"

"Who?" Surely Henry wasn't diseased.

"Chickens! Melissa, I just don't believe it. I don't know what's going on over there, but I can tell you I intend to find out. It may be a disease that's affecting your mind."

"Mother—"

"I suppose I'll just have to come over there and straighten things out myself."

Melissa had been afraid of that. She tried once more. "Things are straight. What's the big deal about a lousy ballet?"

"I knew it. Something has happened. You always loved the ballet."

Actually, Melissa had always hated the ballet. *Henry* had always loved the ballet. "Mother, I'll let you know when the house is ready."

"I will see you very soon, Melissa, ready house or not. I'll tell Henry it's probably the chickens. The disease has temporarily affected your mind."

"Mother!" But the dial tone sounded in her ear. She slumped into her lawn chair, the lovely evening ruined. She knew her mother did not make idle threats. She also knew if her mother ever found out the whole story, she would probably have Melissa committed. Melissa sighed. She would just have to keep her mother away somehow. If Mrs. Talbut ever really got wound up...Melissa couldn't stand up to her.

CHAPTER FIVE

MELISSA GAZED the length of the chicken house, a smile on her face. She'd managed to establish a routine for tending the chicks and discovered she really enjoyed the work. What she enjoyed most was the time alone. No one looked over her shoulder, no one urged her to do things she didn't want to do. Melissa began to see things differently. It had come as a shock to realize that all her life people had been telling her what to do. Worse, she'd listened. She'd always assumed that everyone lived that way, but now she began to experience real doubts.

Melissa hurried through her afternoon chores so she would have time to shower and rest before Dave arrived. She felt her pulse speed up at the thought. Her mother would die if she knew Melissa was entertaining a working man, or any other man for that matter. But Melissa wanted to see him again. She liked the feelings he aroused in her.

Standing in the bare bedroom, she wondered what she should wear and finally decided it didn't really matter. She settled on faded denim jeans, faded at the factory of course, and a yellow cotton shirt.

Wondering about the best place for a picnic, she wandered toward the end of the millpond. Tall, graceful willow trees drooped over the still water. Someone had planted them in a circle, Melissa realized when she discovered the tiny clearing in their midst. Ducking the slender branches, she stepped into the little area. Perfect. Just made for a picnic.

Stepping back out, she resolved that just as soon as the chickens were old enough to take care of themselves for longer periods, she would paint. The house and the millpond and the sunrise. She wanted something to take back with her, something to remember this place and this summer by—and felt a twinge of sadness at the thought of leaving.

She heard the truck before she saw it. Waving, she watched Dave get out of the cab. He wore jeans and a short-sleeved Western shirt, the pale blue making his eyes look darker. As he came closer, she noticed the pearl-headed buttons on the shirt sparkling in the late afternoon sun. He stopped and went back to the truck, returning with a huge basket and a quilt. She watched the easy gait and her blood began to race. He started toward her again.

"Hi."

Suddenly Melissa couldn't think of a thing to say. "Hi." When he just stared at her without speaking, she thought about the place by the willows. "There's a wonderful spot down by those willows. Unless you'd rather..."

His smile dazzled her. "I see you've found the secret place." At her raised eyebrows, he explained. "When we were kids we used to sneak down there, peel our clothes and go skinny-dipping. We were sure the Beadles had no idea what was going on." His laughter seemed to fill the air.

"Skinny-dipping?"

He nodded while his eyes wandered up and down her still figure. "Don't tell me you've never been skinny-dipping!" She shrugged her shoulders slightly. "That's swimming in your birthday suit."

"Naked?" Melissa felt a flush start at the back of her neck. She'd never swam anyplace except a pool.

He smiled. "A very common practice among boys in rural areas." He caught up to her and they ducked under the willow branches into the tiny clearing. "Mrs. Beadle told me years later that they always knew when we came to swim. I was mortified."

Dave set down the basket and spread the quilt on the sandy ground. Melissa reached down to touch it, preferring to think about quilts than about skinny-dipping—particularly about Dave skinny-dipping. "What a beautiful quilt. Who made it?"

"My mother. It's a lone star pattern." The bright colors of the quilt seemed to highlight the pale-green leaves of the willows. Dave motioned Melissa to sit and began to unload the basket. "Meat, cheese and bread from the Ozark Smokehouse." He pulled out a bottle of pale wine, bearing a handwritten label. "Muscadine wine from a friend of mine."

Melissa sat on the far side of the quilt, suddenly feeling very confined and much too close to this man. She watched as he piled layers of meat and cheese on the dark bread, then took the offering along with a glass of the pale wine. She sipped the wine, then giggled. "This tastes like fresh fruit." Melissa seldom drank and the only wine she knew about was what Henry ordered with meals. It was always very dry and tasted vinegary to her.

"Muscadines. It's regional."

Melissa ate the food, not tasting it, conscious only of the return of the butterflies to her stomach. She could feel him watching her eat. A peek over her wineglass confirmed it. He seemed to be tense, and of course that made her tense, too. She told herself to relax, settle down, then the butterflies would go away. When that didn't seem to work, she drank the wine quickly, hoping to drown them. He refilled her glass. After another gulp, she felt a little better. "Have you lived here all your life?"

He nodded and she saw his Adam's apple bob as he swallowed. A butterfly lurched and she took another swallow of the fruity wine. "I've lived in Tulsa all my life."

"Tulsa's nice. Are your parents there?" he asked as he sipped the wine.

"Only my mother. Dad died when I was young. Vietnam." Melissa emptied her glass and held it out for a refill.

"I'm sorry. It must have been tough for your mother and you alone." He pulled two perfect-looking pears from the basket, setting one near her sandwich.

Melissa frowned. "You obviously don't know my mother."

"Do I take it you don't get along too well with her?"

Suddenly Melissa wanted to tell him about her mother and what she'd been feeling this past week. She didn't totally understand those feelings herself, but perhaps it would help to talk about them. "I don't know. I mean I always thought we got along fine. Now I'm not so sure." She swallowed more wine.

His voice was persuasive. "Tell me about it." He chewed the tangy bread, watching her abandon her sandwich for the pear.

Melissa launched into the story, partly to distract herself from those blue eyes that seemed to be everywhere at once. "I've always been sure my mother sacrificed the best years of her life for me. Good schools, the whole thing. I've always believed that was important." She leaned toward him, the mossy-green eyes staring earnestly into his. "Now I'm not so sure. In the past week I've felt...well...maybe she did it because she wanted to." Her voice dropped to a whisper as if she were discussing a conspiracy of some sort. Thoughts boiled in her head. She took another sip of wine. "I mean, I realized yesterday I've never been on my own, until now. I also realized some things have been missing in my life. At least I think they have."

Dave leaned toward the wide green eyes. "But you work, don't you?"

She nodded, feeling very relaxed now. Well, as relaxed as she could feel with him leaning so close. She thought she might drown in those eyes. "But I think my mother probably decided I would become a teacher. *I* don't ever remember deciding that." Melissa sipped the wine, pulling her eyes from his, only to find herself staring at a strong tanned arm. Pale-golden hair curled over the muscle, which rippled as he changed position.

"You don't live with your mother, do you?" He lay back on the quilt, propping himself on one elbow.

Melissa moved a little closer, wondering why he'd abandoned her. "No, but I have a roommate, and Mother seems to be there a lot." She took a healthy sip of the wonderful wine, knowing her mother would disapprove. "It's like I'm just passing time until the next planned phase of my life."

Dave shifted, knowing the man at the auction must be part of that plan. "Marriage?"

Melissa looked crestfallen. "Henry."

"Henry." He looked like a Henry. "Are you going to marry him?"

Melissa nodded, aware that Dave was suddenly holding his breath. She wondered if he was choking. "As soon as he's financially able to support a wife."

That sounded about right. "What does Henry do?"

"Soybeans." Another swig of the fruity liquid and she leaned close again. He still seemed to be holding his breath, his mouth set in a hard line.

"Soybeans." That too figured. "Futures?" At her nod, he continued. "How long have you been engaged?"

"We're not actually engaged. It's more like engaged to be engaged or something. Four years."

"Four years? You've been engaged for four years?" He let out a long sigh.

Melissa nodded sadly, happy that Dave seemed to be breathing again, sad at the thought of her engagement. "Henry believes in long engagements." She waved her glass in his face, and the motion of the air brought a hint of jasmine to his nostrils. "My future is totally dependent on the price of soybeans." She leaned forward until she found herself inches away from a shiny pearl button. Staring at the glossy surface, she shook her head so that her hair brushed his face. "Do you know what that's like?"

Dave reached out, stroking her cheek with the back of a finger. His voice caressed her. "Do you love him?" He watched her face crease into a frown, and knew she did not love Henry.

"I guess, although Mother always said better to marry for security than love." Her eyes met his. "Mother's not too much on love as a basis for a continuing relationship. She says it wears thin soon enough."

"Your mother sounds like a charming lady," he whispered sarcastically. Stroking her cheek again, he lay down flat on the quilt, passing his hand over his eyes. "I can't wait to meet her."

Melissa let her glass slip to the quilt and stretched out, propped on one elbow. She felt very good. "I doubt you'd like her. She's not too much on her daughter mingling with workingmen either." She sat back up, eyes wide, red staining both cheeks. "I didn't mean that the way it sounded." She leaned close again. "You're not insulted, are you? You'd just have to know my mother."

"I think I'll pass if it's all the same." Dave had known mothers like that before. "When are you and Henry supposed to get married?" He raised himself on his elbow.

"Who knows? Another drought or recession and it could be years." Melissa had never talked to anyone this way, but then she'd never had so much wine before. "I'm hoping being away from him this summer will hurry things up. He's very upset about my being here, buying this place and all."

The corners of Dave's mouth twitched and the blue eyes twinkled. "Why should he be upset? It's your money, isn't it?"

Melissa chose to ignore any discussion of why Henry was upset, although she did wonder why Dave thought it was funny. At the moment, she couldn't think of anything funny about Henry. "I have to tell you something, Dave. I don't miss Henry like I think I should."

Dave stroked her hair. "It doesn't sound like there's much to miss. He's crazy to let you run around loose."

Melissa couldn't figure out what was making her so warm all of a sudden. It must be the wine. She retreated slightly, gulping in the cool evening air. "He trusts me. He knows I'll be there when he's ready."

Dave followed her retreat, reaching out to trace her collarbone with a fingertip. "And will you?" He felt her shiver. "Does Henry make you feel like this, Melissa?"

No one had ever made Melissa feel like that, and she liked it. Maybe wine did this to people...after it made them feel warm. Shifting to bring herself a little closer to the magical finger that was now stroking her neck, she looked into his eyes. "Henry is not into physical."

"That figures." His finger trailed up her jawline and behind her ear, gently pulling her closer. "How about you?" The finger continued its journey to her cheek, coming to rest on her full lips. They felt soft and warm. He leaned closer and gently touched her lips with his.

"I'm sure the physical side is vastly overrated." Melissa sighed. She wasn't sure of anything now except that his lips made her tingle all over. When his lips touched hers again, she knew there was more to life than Henry had led her to believe.

"Are you sure about that, Melissa?" He trailed kisses down her neck to the hollow of her throat.

Melissa felt a wave of heat start deep within her and spread like a fire on a windy day. He found her lips again, the kiss more insistent this time. The heat spread, scaring her. All her mother's warnings flooded into her brain, threatening to smother the fire. She shouldn't be doing this. Yet...she had to think about this. "Would you like some coffee?"

Dave's eyes closed. He knew she had encountered some inner barrier. He bit down hard on his lip. "Coffee. Why not?" He gathered up the basket and quilt and followed her to the house.

Dave flopped down in one of the lawn chairs, watching her look into each box of chicks on her way to the kitchen. "How are your little charges doing?"

"Much better, thank you. I think most of them will be able to go back to the flock soon." She busied herself with the coffee, somewhat embarrassed by what had happened between them. She also felt a little tipsy.

"That's nice." Dave watched her busy herself around the kitchen, stopping several times to raise a box cover and peek in. "You should get a dog to keep you company and protect you."

Melissa carried in two steaming mugs of coffee, carefully threading her way through the boxes. "Do you think I could get one? I've always wanted a dog, ever since I can remember." She wondered at the sudden change of subject. She'd felt his eyes on her as she fixed the coffee, but now, as she looked at him, his face was closed, the eyes unreadable. But dogs seemed a safe enough subject.

Dave shot her a look of surprise. "You've never had a dog?" Through his mind's eye marched the long line of faithful companions who had escorted him into manhood. Every kid should have a dog. Then he frowned as he remembered Alicia's reaction to the thought of a dog on her expensive white carpet.

"Mother thinks they're dirty and smelly." She settled into the lawn chair facing him, carefully looking at the coffee in her cup.

Mother *would* think they're dirty. Dave felt stirrings of dislike for this mother he'd never met. "They're a lot of company. Better than most people I know."

Melissa studied her coffee a little longer, then brightened. A dog. Why shouldn't she have a dog? "Maybe I will get one." Her head began to clear as she sipped the hot coffee, but she didn't regret anything she'd told Dave. Sitting there, she began to feel something like resentment toward her mother, something she'd never experienced before. She imagined she'd heard resentment in Dave's voice.

Dave began to tell stories about the various animals of his youth, and Melissa got an inkling of something else she'd missed. It was becoming more apparent she had a lot of catching up to do. She watched the lanky form stretched out in the chair, her pulse beating just a little faster as she studied him. The shrill ring of the phone brought her back to reality.

Melissa knew it had to be either Henry or her mother, and she didn't really want to talk to either of them right now. "Hello?"

Her mother's voice seemed to fill the room. "Melissa, nice girls do not break their mother's hearts. You've simply got to come home. I can't imagine what you can possibly find interesting in that godforsaken place, but Henry and I are worried sick about you."

Melissa's voice grew smaller. The call yesterday had just been a fishing expedition. This one was the beginning of a full-scale battle plan. "Mother, I'm just fine."

"Are you coming home this weekend?"

Melissa took a deep breath and looked at Dave. "No, I'm busy with the house."

"That's just what Henry told me you would say. Only yesterday it was chickens. Well, in that case, we're driving over on Saturday."

Melissa's eyes grew wide. "Mother, you can't."

"I beg your pardon, young lady."

"I mean the house isn't ready."

"Nonsense. Perhaps we can talk some sense into that head of yours. We'll be there on Saturday."

Melissa replaced the phone, looking totally dejected. Dave stood, walked over and gathered her into his arms. She came willingly. "They don't know about the farm or the chickens, do they?"

She shook her head and burrowed deeper into his chest. Her voice when it came sounded muffled.

"They think I just bought a house." She raised her head and frowned. "How did you know?"

"It wasn't hard to figure out. Besides, Mr. Felker was quite upset with you. He was afraid you were going to faint in his bank or something awful."

Melissa reddened at the thought that Mr. Felker had told Dave the whole sordid tale. Dave must think her a total dimwit. "Oh. Mother will probably kill me."

Dave's anger flared at the unknown woman. "Melissa, you're a grown person, free to do what you want. You just have to realize that before you can use that freedom." He tipped back her chin and made her look at him. "It's your money and it's none of their business."

Melissa pulled back. "You don't understand. You don't know my mother."

"No, Melissa, I don't, but I'm beginning to know *you* and I think you want to be your own person. You just don't know how." His voice caressed her once more. "Let me help."

Melissa turned and flopped down into the chair again. How could he possibly understand? "Face it. My mother raised a wimp."

"Melissa. Start now. Tell them to bug off."

She looked up in shock. "I can't tell my own mother to bug off. You just don't understand. I'll just have to work it out."

She was saved from further explanation by the telephone. Of course, that would be Henry. "Yes, Henry?"

A pause. "How did you know?"

"I just knew."

"Your mother and I are coming over Saturday."

"I know." Melissa made a face at Dave.

"How did you know? We just decided." The voice sounded at the edge of exasperation.

"Mother called."

"Oh. She and I are going to the ballet."

"That's nice." Better her than me.

"Melissa, I must say you don't seem to have much to say to me."

"I'm tired."

"What could you possibly be tired from? Surely not a few stupid chickens."

Tired from soybeans? Why not tired from chickens? Melissa looked at all the boxes. If Henry only knew. "You'd be surprised, Henry."

"This is a depressing conversation, Melissa. I hope you can do better on Saturday."

"I don't suppose there's any chance of talking you out of coming." Or maybe the moon would fall out of the sky.

"Your mother is adamant. She's even worried about some disease. And I'm adamant. This thing has gone far enough."

The adamant twins. "Good night, Henry."

"Melissa—"

She replaced the receiver on the strangled cry and turned to look at Dave. He seemed to be fuming. "What is this? Laurel and Hardy pick on Melissa?"

Melissa sighed. Why did everyone have to have explanations? "They're coming Saturday. For sure."

Dave pulled her close, stroking her hair. "Do they keep that closely in touch with each other?"

Melissa tried to laugh. "Well, the calls do seem to come in pairs. I think it's called 'Save Melissa From Herself,' or something."

"Oh, honey. I know it's tough on you. But hang in there. I might be able to help, you know." He raged at the sight of the sad, worried little girl who moments before had been an animated, lovely woman.

"Uh . . . I don't think you can help. You just don't understand." Melissa could tell he was angry, but failed to see why her mother and Henry should matter one way or the other to him.

"You may think I don't understand, but I expect I'll understand come Saturday." A grin suddenly lit up his whole face. "Okay. I'll see you tomorrow." He kissed her, lingering only a moment.

She waved after him, wondering what had suddenly cheered him so. She couldn't think of one thing to be cheery about at this moment. Dave was very handsome when he smiled, she thought. But why his sudden change from anger to a grin, almost as if a light bulb had gone on somewhere in his mind? That would give Melissa something else to worry about. She'd already started worrying about Saturday.

CHAPTER SIX

DAVE GIRDED HIS LOINS and walked into the county dog pound. He hated the place, but knew the dog he sought was probably waiting there. An older woman hurried toward him. "May I help you?"

"I'm looking for a dog. Is it okay if I just look around?" Dave had decided during the long restless night that Melissa would have the dog she'd always wanted.

"Certainly. We have some nice dogs this week." Her meaning was unmistakable. Those dogs probably wouldn't be there next week. "Any particular breed? The runs are through that door. Let me know if any of them interests you."

He walked through the door and immediately the clamor started. Dogs of every size and conceivable variety rushed to the wire doors, begging for attention. He stopped and petted a few through the wire, but continued to scan the runs for the dog he wanted. At the last cage, he saw her. She obviously wanted no part of him or any other human being.

About the size of a cocker spaniel, she looked like thousands of other dogs in rural America. A farm dog of the type so common as to be almost a breed. Long black hair, matted and dull. Tan legs and tan spots for eyebrows that gave her a perpetually worried look. She stood at the back of the run, stiff-legged, eyes displaying the lack of trust she felt toward the human race.

Dave knelt in front of the cage, watching, talking softly. "You've had a hard time of it, haven't you, girl?" The dog gave no response, but the sad eyes watched his every move. Her profile indicated recent motherhood. The black tail curled up between her legs. As he shifted his weight to the other foot, he heard a tiny growl. Dave knew this kind of dog. She would be slow to trust, but when it came it would be a fiercely loyal trust that would bond her to her master, or mistress in this case, for life.

This was a creature who would need Melissa and accept her without reservation. And somehow, he knew, she would learn to trust Melissa.

He walked to the front. "I found one I'll take, ma'am."

The woman smiled delightedly and walked back to the runs with him. When he indicated his choice, she frowned. "Are you sure? We haven't been able to do much with her. She just won't have anything to do with people."

"She's certainly wary. But yes, I'm sure." The woman opened the run and Dave stepped in slowly, advancing toward the dog, talking slowly. She made no move to escape and her only response when he picked her up was to tremble. He gave the woman a donation and carried his trembling burden to the truck.

Talking all the time, he put her in the seat. She scooted to the far side and continued to stare at him. He knew this dog had to find her own peace and could not be pushed. He smiled and continued his soft monologue.

When he got to the farm, Melissa was coming down from the chicken house, auburn hair shining in the afternoon sun. It seemed at that moment as though she came striding out of the sun.

Melissa saw him from halfway down the hill. He stood ramrod straight, watching her, cap bill pulled low over his eyes. She hadn't expected him, but her heart raced at the sight, wondering why he'd come. She ran toward him with a smile.

Dave gathered up his furry burden from the truck and turned to her. "I've brought you something." He set the dog down on the grass.

Melissa looked at the trembling wad of fur, her eyes growing wide. She dropped to the grass in a fluid motion, several feet from the dog. "Well, you've had a pretty hard time haven't you, girl?" She made no move to touch the dog, figuring this frightened creature was no different from a frightened child. She'd discovered early on that children needed to make the first move. The dog continued to watch them, distrust evident in her eyes. "Where did you find her? She's beautiful."

He laughed, delighted that she could see past the dog's obvious shortcomings. "She's not much to look at, but give her some time and food and love, and she'll be okay." He was pleased that Melissa had the innate sense not to force herself on the dog, confirming once more that she was a sensitive woman.

"Well, I think we can handle that, can't we, Lady?" Melissa looked up to thank him, then stopped as their eyes met. She saw a play of emotions cross his face, emotions she couldn't begin to fathom.

"Lady?" His gaze returned to the dog.

"Of course. That's what she is, a lady fallen on hard times. I'll have to get some dog food."

"Already got it." He retrieved a sack from the truck.

"Let's have some supper, Lady. Come on." She headed to the house, followed by Dave and the dog. Lady stopped to investigate the boxes of chickens, then trailed into the kitchen. She sat and looked at the bowl of food, watching Melissa. When they left the room, they heard frantic gulping and licking. They watched as she came into the living room, looked around, then lay down in a corner where she could observe them both.

Melissa smiled and shivered. "Thank you. Why did you bring her?"

Dave shrugged. "Everyone should have a dog sometime in his life. Besides, she'll be protection for you here alone. And she needs a home."

"I'll take extra good care of her."

Dave followed Melissa's eyes as she glanced toward the dog. "I know you will. What will your mother think of her?" He felt certain that thought had not occurred to Melissa yet.

"She'll hate her. And she's coming tomorrow with Henry unless I can figure out a way to stop them." She didn't even want to think about Saturday.

Dave frowned. "Melissa, why can't you just tell them not to come?"

"Because it wouldn't make any difference. They'd come anyway. Mother and Henry think I need looking after." She slumped a little farther down in the chair.

"Do you?" Dave sat rigidly in the other chair.

"I don't think so. Maybe I never did, or maybe I did once and don't now. I don't know. It's all so confusing. I just want them to leave me alone until I get things straightened out." She looked up. "I'm happy here. I even like taking care of the chickens. But they'll convince me I'm crazy or something." She noticed Dave's tension and wondered if he wanted her to go through all the explanations again. He was probably one of those people who thought talking about things helped. Melissa subscribed to the theory that running away was more useful.

He reached over and took her hand. "Can I help?"

She felt her hand burn and her eyes grew wide. "Oh, I don't think it would be a good idea for you to be around while they're here."

He knew the answer, but asked the question anyway. "Why? Because I'm not quite in the same circle?"

"Oh no, it's just that..." She looked at him, something new in her eyes. "Actually I guess that's exactly the reason. That's awful, that's really awful. I guess I'm no better than my mother." She put her elbows on her knees, and he caught her scent. The mixture of jasmine and chickens brought a smile to his lips. It seemed a wonderful combination. "Dave, I don't think I want to be like her."

He pulled her chin up to face him. "Then don't. Be what you want to be, Melissa."

Melissa knew he was going to kiss her. A voice somewhere told her he shouldn't, but she didn't resist. This man offered something that had been heretofore unknown to her—a chance to be someone different. He seemed to think she could be different; she wasn't so sure, but she felt drawn to him in that moment. And then there were the tingling feelings beginning to course through her body again. She leaned toward him. When his lips touched hers, a warm fuzzy feeling replaced the tingling. His lips were gentle and undemanding, and she responded.

He dropped to the floor and knelt before her. His hands buried themselves in her thick hair. "Melissa, you're a beautiful, intelligent, lovely woman. You don't need the Terrible Twins running your life."

Melissa giggled at the image of Henry and her mother being twins. Then without thinking, her hands went to the thick yellow mane of his hair and she marveled at the feel of it. Melissa wrapped her arms around the muscled body and her fingers felt the muscles quiver at her touch. She sensed warmth and safety here. Dave treated her like a woman, not some errant child. Nothing like this had ever happened to Melissa before, but she responded instinctively.

Then his mouth traced a line toward her ear and she heard a moan, unsure if she'd made the sound. She wondered at the strength in his arms as he pulled her closer, feeling his hard body against hers. The coarse blond hairs tickled her throat and she wanted to feel his skin. Her hands slipped into the shirt, causing him to shake. She felt rather than heard his voice in her ear. "Oh, Melissa, where have you been all my life?"

Melissa trembled, wanting him to quench the fire that was spreading through her.

"Melissa, we'll get through it together."

The words seemed to shatter her fantasy and smother the fire. There was no "we." He sounded as if... as if they were somehow in league against her mother and Henry. Maybe he would be her next guardian. That scared her. Her feelings scared her. She felt inadequate. "Dave, I'm not very good at this."

"Melissa, you're wonderful. If you were any better, I couldn't stand it." But he felt her pull back and he sat back on his heels.

"We shouldn't do this. It's wrong." Her mother's voice sounded in her head.

His voice was sharp. "It's not wrong, Melissa. Don't ever say that. What I feel for you is right, honey, more right than anything I've ever felt in my life."

"It can't be. We're strangers." Melissa couldn't think of anything better to say, knowing she couldn't tell him her mother wouldn't approve. And she wasn't about to tell him just how scared she was of... everything.

He reached over and his mouth found hers, still gentle this time, but also demanding. She felt the fire start again. He pulled away then and forced her to look at him. "You feel the same things I feel. You just won't admit it." Her head shook. "Melissa, look at me and tell me you don't feel what's between us."

Melissa felt it even now. "But I'm engaged to Henry," she wailed.

"Engaged to be engaged. There is a difference." He rubbed his jaw viciously, then took a deep breath. "Melissa, do you feel that way when Henry touches you? I don't think so, because you know deep down that you don't love Henry and he doesn't love you or he wouldn't put soybeans ahead of you. I know what's inside you, waiting to come out, and I think you know, too. And before this summer is done, you will know that love doesn't require a month or a year. What's there is there. And you'll know. And that's a promise."

"But..."

"No ifs, ands, or buts. If you felt that way about Henry, you'd have been married long ago. Am I right?"

Melissa pulled away from the intense blue eyes and looked at the floor. She'd never felt much of anything with Henry, just secure, but she wasn't about to admit it to a man who set fire to her body with a touch. She felt emotions at war within her—and confusion. Dave seemed to make things more complicated than they already were.

She touched her lips, still soft and warm from his kisses. She didn't want to think about what he said, or about her feelings. She never talked about feelings, and she certainly didn't want to think about Henry. She wanted to feel warm and fuzzy again without having to think about all those complications. So she fell back on her usual method of dealing with feelings, perfected over the years, and changed the subject. "Do you know how to paint a house?" She looked at him, her eyes a picture of innocence.

He stared at her for a long moment, then sat back on the floor, laughing and shaking his head. "Paint a house? I assume we're changing the subject to avoid talking about how we feel?"

Melissa blushed at his perceptiveness. She shook her head. Why did he have to be so smart? "No, of course not. I just thought I'd start painting the house tomorrow, and I really don't know where to begin."

"Right. Paint the house. I think I can handle that. When did you want to do it?" He suppressed the grin he felt inside.

"In the morning?" She wished his mouth would stop twitching, although it was better than that intense stare.

"Why not? Of course, I could stay here tonight and get an early start." He watched her cheeks redden again.

"Uh . . . I don't have a bed."

He stood and pulled her up. "Joke. I'll be here around nine. Do you have the paint?"

"I'll get it in the morning. Early." She was aware of his nearness and started feeling very warm again.

His laughter filled the room. "That's because you actually had no intention of painting the house tomorrow, right?"

"Well . . ."

"It's okay, sweet. I do understand, probably better than you'll ever know." He kissed her until she thought she would melt. "But those feelings are not going to go away just because you try to ignore them. And I'm not going away either, so you might as well get used to it." He saw her take a deep breath. "See you tomorrow. And take care of the lady."

Melissa watched him leave, confusion growing within her. She turned to the black dog who was eyeing her from the corner. "You want to go meet the chickens, Lady?" She left the house noting that Lady stayed well behind, but followed nevertheless.

She kept up her monologue. "Why do things have to be so complicated, Lady? I'm going through life, minding my own business, everything planned. Then I go to one lousy farm auction and all of a sudden I'm in hock up to my neck, I have thousands of babies to tend to, a man who makes me feel funny all over and a dog who's old before her time." She turned to look at the silent, scruffy animal following her and felt the tug at her heartstrings. "And right now, you're the best part of the whole deal."

She quickly made her rounds in the chicken house, the dog following, stopping only to stare at the chicks. Melissa fed and watered them automatically, her thoughts on Dave Winston. She suspected he might be more than just another working man. He was intelligent, obviously well educated, and something else ... she couldn't put her finger on what. All she could put her finger on was the fact that she had some very strong feelings about him, and that meant more trouble for her—as if she didn't have trouble enough. She couldn't believe she could develop such strong feelings for someone in such a short time.

Gertie was sitting on the porch when she came back from the chicken house. Somehow, the sight of her neighbor just sitting there in the late afternoon made Melissa relax. She hurried toward that island of peace and sanity. "Hi, Gertie."

"Figured you were tendin' the chicks. How they doin'?" She craned her neck to look at a stiff-legged Lady, who was pressing against Melissa's legs and

Yes, become a Harlequin home subscriber and the celebration goes on forever.

To begin with we'll send you:

- **4 new Harlequin Romance novels — Free**
- **an elegant, purse-size manicure set — Free**
- **and an exciting mystery bonus — Free**

And that's not all! Special extras — Three more reasons to celebrate

4. Money-Saving Home Delivery That's right! When you become a Harlequin home subscriber the excitement, romance and far-away adventures of Harlequin Romance novels can be yours for previewing in the convenience of your own home **at less than retail prices.** Here's how it works. Every month we'll deliver six new books right to your door. If you decide to keep them, they'll be yours for only $1.75! That's 20¢ less per book than what you pay in stores. And there is **no charge for shipping and handling.**

5. Free Monthly Newsletter — It's "Heart to Heart" — **the** indispensable insider's look at our most popular writers and their up-coming novels. Now you can have a behind-the-scenes look at the fascinating world of Harlequin! It's an added bonus you'll look forward to every month!

6. More Surprise Gifts — Because our home subscribers are our most valued readers, we'll be sending you additional free gifts from time to time — as a token of our appreciation.

*This beautiful manicure set will be a useful and elegant item to carry in your handbag. Its rich burgundy case is a perfect expression of your style and good taste. And it's yours **free** in this amazing Harlequin celebration!*

HARLEQUIN READER SERVICE
FREE OFFER CARD

4 FREE BOOKS

ELEGANT MANICURE SET – FREE

FREE MYSTERY BONUS

PLACE YOUR BALLOON STICKER HERE!

MONEY SAVING HOME DELIVERY

FREE FACT-FILLED NEWSLETTER

MORE SURPRISE GIFTS THROUGHOUT THE YEAR – FREE

☐ **YES!** Please send me my four Harlequin Romance novels **Free**, along with my manicure set and my **free mystery gift**. Then send me six new Harlequin Romance novels every month and bill me just $1.75 per book (20¢ less than retail), with no extra charges for shipping and handling. If I am not completely satisfied, I may return a shipment and cancel at any time. **The free books, manicure set and mystery gift remain mine to keep.**

316 CIR VDET

FIRST NAME _____ LAST NAME _____

(PLEASE PRINT)

ADDRESS _____ APT. _____

CITY _____ PROV./STATE _____

POSTAL CODE / ZIP _____

HARLEQUIN "NO RISK GUARANTEE"
• There is no obligation to buy – the free books and gifts remain yours to keep.
• You pay the lowest price possible – and receive books before they're available in stores.
• You may end your subscription anytime-just let us know.

PRINTED IN U.S.A.

Remember! To receive your four free books, manicure set and surprise mystery bonus return the postpaid card below. But don't delay!

DETACH & MAIL CARD TODAY

If card has been removed, write to:
Harlequin Reader Service, P.O. Box 609, Fort Erie, Ontario L2A 9Z9

Business Reply Mail

No Postage Stamp
Necessary if Mailed
in Canada

Postage will be paid by

Harlequin Reader Service
P.O. Box 609
Fort Erie, Ontario
L2A 9Z9

Canada Post
Postes Canada
708

emitting low growling noises. "My Lord, where'd you get that?"

Melissa reached down to calm the dog. "Isn't she wonderful? A friend gave her to me."

"Looks like your friend got dumped."

"Dumped?"

Gertie leaned back and shook her head. "I can't begin to count the number of pitiful creatures like that one who've been dumped on this road. I used to try and take care of all of them, but there is a limit to the number of hungry faces a body can face every morning. I just can't understand why people do it."

Melissa didn't at all like the thought of people just taking their dogs out to the country and dumping them. She guessed she'd never really thought about it. "Oh, this one wasn't dumped here. My friend got her somewhere."

"That's even worse. Lord, if you're goin' lookin' for one, seems like you could find a better specimen than that."

"I think she's wonderful."

Gertie stood up. "Well, if that's what you think, then that's what she'll be. Just get a little meat on her bones. Anyhow, what I came for was to tell you you're welcome to some furniture. Come by when you have the time and we'll see what we can find." She grinned at Melissa. "Also, I wondered how your house chicks were comin' along."

"Come see for yourself. I've only lost three."

Gertie surveyed the boxes, stopping to peer into a few. "Good for you. They'll make it. Well, I'll be on my way."

"Thanks, Gertie. I'll see you soon." Melissa watched the older woman head home, thinking how much she liked Gertie. Gertie didn't laugh or lecture, she just accepted her. Melissa liked that a lot.

She ate a sandwich for supper, paying little attention to the food. After a hot bath, she settled down in her sleeping bag. As she stretched out on the hard floor, she vowed she would take Gertie up on her offer very soon. Probably the attic would have ten of everything, but no bed. At the thought of a bed, she thought again of Dave. She blushed in the darkness, wondering what on earth was happening to her. As her thoughts went back to the afternoon, the warm fuzzy feeling returned. She lay quiet, willing sleep to come, but her body replayed the sensations he'd caused.

Lady had bedded down in the corner on a towel, so she provided no distraction at all. Melissa knew, lying in the quiet, that she had two choices—either give in to her feelings about Dave, or stay away from him. Obviously he was a very determined man. She would have to opt for keeping him at arm's length from now on. She wondered if that was far enough.

Melissa finally forced her mind to blank out the rampant thoughts and feelings and relax. She'd dozed when a cold nose touched her neck very lightly. She smiled, but didn't move, afraid she would frighten the dog. Then she felt the skinny body drop at her back and heard a long sigh. Melissa knew then that the dog would be all right, and that she trusted her new owner. She'd made the first move. Melissa closed her eyes and murmured softly, "It's you and me against the world, Lady."

CHAPTER SEVEN

MELISSA WOKE in the early light of morning with the dog still curled against her back. As she stretched and consciousness began to take hold, she groaned. This was definitely not going to be a good day. Staggering to the kitchen, Lady at her heels, she put the water on to boil. This was going to be a full-pot morning.

After her morning routine in the bath, she poured the first cup of strong coffee and returned to the living room. She had to go get the lousy paint. "I had no intention of painting the house today, Lady. I guess that will teach me not to change the subject with whatever pops into my mind." Lady just watched, keeping her own counsel. Melissa quickly began to plot her strategy to get through the day. She would go get the paint, she and Dave would paint for a while, then she would get rid of him. She couldn't take a chance that Henry and her mother would come driving in and find them up to their eyes in paint. She wasn't up to explaining that. Knowing her mother, their arrival should be about midafternoon.

She got a second cup of coffee, feeling better now that the caffeine coursed through her body. That would give her time to sort through all the chickens in their boxes. She could take the ones that were well enough back to the big house and condense the remaining ones to a few boxes. Those she would put in the barn for the afternoon. That way, given a little luck, they would never know there was a chicken on the place. No, that wouldn't work, she'd told them she had baby chicks. She'd better keep one box in the house for effect. She sighed and reached down to stroke the dog. "I won't put you in the barn, though. They'll just have to accept you. Come on, let's go do our chores." She started up the hill, the dog close behind. It was absurd to have to go through all this. After all, they were her chickens. She had screwed up and got the chickens fair and square. She knew her mother would never spend the night in a house with no beds, so she wouldn't have to worry about them staying over. Assuming she could shuffle everything on schedule she should be okay. The way the day was going, that was a big assumption.

She quickly went through the routine. The chicks barely showed yellow down now, and had begun to eat and drink from the bigger equipment. They weren't nearly as cute, but they sure were a lot less work. She was pleased with how they were growing. Actually she was quite pleased with her new life, if she could only get through this day. Perhaps she would fall in a bucket of paint and drown. Then she wouldn't have to deal with any of it.

She returned to the house, gulped down more coffee, then decided she'd better get the paint. Lady followed her to the car but refused to get in. "Been on one too many car rides, huh? Come on, now. I'm not going to dump you anywhere." She finally lifted the dog into the car. Lady sat against the far door, eyeing her suspiciously.

Melissa came out of the hardware store loaded down with paint, brushes, scrapers and numerous other articles the man had assured her were essential items for painting a house. She hoped Dave would know what to do with them. When she drove in, he was sitting on the top step, leaning against the porch railing. Melissa's heart pounded at the sight of him in the faded jeans and snug white T-shirt. As he walked over to help unload the car, she caught a whiff of soap and after-shave. Her heart pounded even faster, and she knew the day was not going as planned. "Hi."

Dave flashed her a crooked grin, knowing full well she didn't want to paint the house today, knowing also that she would have to get rid of him before the Tulsa contingent arrived. He carried the buckets of paint to the side of the house. "Ready to get started?"

She ducked around him with her load. "As ready as I'll ever be."

He grinned at her back. "Hey, it was your idea."

"Don't remind me." She dumped the sack of unidentifiable tools on the porch. "Do you have any idea what all these things are?"

He leaned over her. "I think I can handle most of them. I assume you've never painted a house before."

Melissa was already in a bad mood from trying to figure out the logistics for the day. Added to that was the tenseness she felt when she got close to this man. As a result Melissa wasn't in any mood to talk about her shortcomings as a house painter. "It can't be that hard."

"Kind of like the chickens?"

"Well, you have to admit the chickens are doing well. At least the house isn't going to die or anything if we screw up."

His head went back and laughter seemed to echo through the valley. "I guess if you look at it that way, we're on safe ground."

"I'm glad you find this amusing. I have to tell you I don't think this is going to be my day." She stood, hands on her hips, looking disgusted with the whole project. "So what do we do first?"

Dave very carefully opened two gallons of paint, not showing any surprise at the rather bright yellow color. "Nice color." He handed her a brush and one of the buckets. "I found a ladder in the barn. I'll paint high, you paint low." He watched as she moved to the corner of the house. "Sure you don't need any instruction?"

Melissa glared at him and plunged the brush into the paint. She held the brush as if it were a club and furiously swabbed the paint on the siding. After about the third dip into the bucket, paint began to drip back over the handle and run down her arm. And of course her nose itched. She glanced up at Dave's arm making clean sure strokes and saw with dismay that his boards looked nice and smooth and hers looked ...globby. Attacking the siding again, her only reward was more paint running down her arm and cold, wet spots of paint on her face, the result of slapping the brush a little too hard. Perhaps there was more to this than met the eye. She didn't want to ask him to show her how to do it, but on the other hand she didn't want her little house to look globby. Probably he'd given her a bad brush.

She eyed his area again, then hers. "Uh, how come paint is running down my brush?"

Dave glanced down, biting his lip to stop himself from laughing at the sight. She stood defiantly staring up at him, face spattered with bright yellow spots, paint creating a yellow pathway down her arm to drip from her elbow. He willed himself to look serious. "It's just a matter of technique. Would you like me to give you a few pointers?" She was certainly showing promising signs of independence this morning.

She glared, but nodded, wondering how he could possibly be so delighted about painting a house.

He climbed down, picking up a rag he'd found in the barn. Carefully wiping the worst of the paint off her arm and the brush, he dipped it lightly in the paint and placed it in her hand. "You have to hold the brush right." His hand closed over hers and he stepped closer until her back brushed his chest. He choked off a sharp breath as their bodies touched. His cheek brushed her hair. He guided her hand in a long stroking motion. "This is real wood siding, so you have to get the paint into the wood, not just on the surface."

Melissa's hand burned under his and nothing existed now except the motion of the brush and the motion of her shoulder rubbing against his hard chest. Her eyes followed the brush, watching the bright yellow color spread. She felt his breath move her hair. The fire began deep within her and she leaned back to press against him. The bright yellow seemed to change, catching fire with her.

She heard him gasp when she leaned back and turned to look at him. But he seemed to be concentrating very hard on the motion of the brush. Her back rubbed against his chest with each movement, and Melissa felt the hard stomach muscles quiver each time she leaned into him. He pulled her closer and time stood still. Only the fire within her and the body touching her existed. The brush, dry now, moving hypnotically deepened her trance. She felt his lips brush her neck and shivered. The fire raged, something she'd never experienced before. It threatened to consume her, and she knew instinctively only this man could quench it.

Dave's hand stroked her back, and she pulled her eyes away from the brush to turn to him. His face was closed, but she saw the desire burning bright in his eyes. She dropped the brush and tilted up her head, waiting for his kiss.

His eyes met hers for a moment, then he stepped away. His voice sounded ragged. "Got it?"

Melissa felt abandoned. She stared at the bright-yellow house, wondering how long they'd been there. The fire deep within her smouldered now, and Melissa wondered anew at the feelings this man aroused in her. And she knew at that moment that one day soon, they would not stop. "Yes. I think I've got it," her voice squeaked. She picked up the brush and started back over her globby patch, again hypnotized both by the brush and by her feelings. She sneaked a glance at Dave, watching his long, almost angry strokes. Melissa sighed and returned to her painting. What was he mad about now?

Dave climbed the ladder and began to paint with a vengeance. He forced all his feelings and his energies into the brush. His concentration finally broke as Lady began to bark frantically. He turned to see a large car drive in. He smiled. A quick glance at Melissa caught shock on her face.

"Oh Lord, they weren't supposed to be here till this afternoon!" Her huge eyes turned upward. "You've got to get out of here." Melissa stood rooted in feelings and emotions, unable to break the spell. Only the sight of her mother getting out of the car spurred her to action.

No way, sweetheart, he thought. "I'll just keep painting. Tell them I'm a hired hand."

"Good idea." She dropped the brush and hurried forward, her main objective now to keep them out of the house. The day was shaping up as she'd known it would—total disaster. She glanced longingly into the paint bucket, wondering if she could get her head in far enough to drown. "I thought you wouldn't be here until later." She noticed the shocked expressions as Henry and her mother stepped out of the car.

Evelyn Talbut was slightly over fifty and had a look of authority. She also had the look of a battleship leading the way into action. Although she was a large woman, she wasn't really that large. It was just the effect she seemed to have on people, especially those who had been swept under by the wake. But this morning, the battleship faltered. Evelyn Talbut was momentarily scuttled as she stared at the paint-streaked creature before her. It couldn't possibly be her daughter. Her hand flew to her ample bosom and she gasped.

"Mother, are you all right?" Melissa had never seen her mother at a loss for words. Then she remembered the paint. "I'm painting the house."

Henry's voice broke in. "I would say that's rather obvious, Melissa. The question is why?" He moved away from the car only to be intercepted by a growling Lady. He stopped, staring at the pitiful creature in his path. "Good grief, what is that?"

Melissa's momentary shock was replaced by a twinge of anger. "It's a dog. She lives with me. Her name is Lady."

Evelyn seemed to have recovered somewhat. "Well really, Melissa. I can't believe this. Look at yourself!"

Melissa did just that, seeing rather a lot of paint, but otherwise just herself. "Painting's messy," she said lamely, the authority in her mother's voice having its usual effect.

"There are people who paint houses for a living, my dear. I can't imagine why you want to do it yourself."

Henry tried to ignore the snarling mess of fur at his feet. "It's all part of her pastoral scene, Evelyn."

They started toward the house. "I hope you have some coffee, Melissa. I'm exhausted. Come, Henry."

Melissa moved to intercept them, remembering the chickens in the house. "Uh...don't go into the house."

Her mother frowned. "Really, Melissa you are behaving in a most peculiar manner. Of course we're going into the house. Why else would we have come?"

Melissa thought they'd come to drag her back, but didn't mention it. "Well, I don't have any furniture yet. Why don't you sit on the porch and I'll bring the coffee?" She heard a choking sound from the ladder and glared over her shoulder.

But the battleship was under full steam, and Melissa knew there was no stopping it now. "Nonsense, Melissa." Her mother sailed up the steps, Henry and Melissa in her wake. She flung open the door and swept in. Immediately she found her progress impeded by boxes—a sea of cardboard boxes—cardboard boxes that made noise. She delicately reached down and removed the towel from the nearest box. The inhabitants immediately began cheeping, setting off cheeping from all the other boxes. Evelyn stood up, both hands flying to her bosom this time. "I think I'm having a heart attack." She plowed her way to a lawn chair. "Melissa, I certainly hope you can explain this."

"They're chickens, Mother."

"I can see that. What the hell are you doing with a house full of chickens?"

Melissa stared in shock. She'd never heard her mother curse. She knew she was in a lot of trouble now. "Actually it's a long story."

"Don't tell me. I don't want to know. Henry, where are you? Disease. That fool of a doctor said it wasn't likely, but of course he didn't know she had legions of them in the house." Evelyn rummaged through her suitcaselike bag and immediately clapped a lace handkerchief to her nose.

The door opened and Henry stalked in, dragging Lady, firmly attached to his pant leg. "Melissa, get this sorry excuse for a dog off me." Melissa retrieved the dog, who continued to growl at him. Then Henry looked around. "My God. Chickens." The last word denoted something akin to the black plague. Melissa had known Henry wouldn't like chickens. She also realized it would be useless to explain to her mother that she wasn't going to catch something from the chicks.

Melissa headed for the kitchen, hoping coffee might defuse the situation. She knew she should have hidden the chickens. She knew that as soon as the shock wore off, they would begin to pressure her, demand she return home. She didn't want to go home, but the question of whether she could stand up to both of them hung heavy. She carried coffee back to the living room, noticing that both Henry and her mother tried to sit so that their feet didn't touch the floor. Lady had resumed her post at Henry's feet, lips curled back to expose shiny white teeth. Since there were only two chairs, Melissa stood leaning against the wall, trying to look nonchalant. A heavy silence descended, broken only by an occasional cheep. She knew the storm was coming.

Evelyn opened her mouth to speak just as the door opened. Dave came in, smiling at everyone and walked over to plant a noisy wet kiss on Melissa's cheek. "Lissy honey, I sure could do with a cuppa coffee." Dave felt the strain on his nostrils as he kept them pinched together to produce the nasal substandard southern mountain dialect he was aiming for. One look at their faces told him he'd succeeded. He gave them a moronic lopsided grin just for good measure. Melissa stared in shock at the strange sounds.

Dave treated her mother to another lopsided grin. "You must be Lissy's momma." He reached over to wring her hand. "You sure raised a mighty fine little ol' gal here." He poked Melissa in the ribs. "Mighty purty, too." He turned to Henry. "And you must be Henry. You sure must be some stallion to let this purty little thing run around by herself." He grabbed Henry's hand and began to exert pressure as he pumped it, enjoying the look of pain on Henry's face. He reluctantly stopped short of bringing Henry to his knees.

Melissa stared in shock at Dave. She didn't even recognize him. He sounded like the man at the feed store. She couldn't imagine why he was acting this way, but she didn't have time to worry about it. She had to get things under control. Almost laughing at that prospect, she looked at Henry. Stallion? She'd thought many things about Henry, but stallion was not one of them. Right now, he looked more like a very wet, very mad old hen. She smiled at her mother, who seemed to be regaining her senses.

"And just who are you, young man?"

"He paints houses, Mother."

Dave wondered how long he could keep up the nasal tone. "Actually I'm a chicken catcher."

Henry and Evelyn cried in unison. "Chicken catcher?"

"Yes ma'am. We go out catch chickens in the big houses. Like the one Lissy has on top of the hill."

Melissa glared at him and kicked him in the shins, feeling momentary satisfaction when he grunted in pain.

Evelyn clutched her bosom with one hand, her lace hankie with the other. "More chickens? On top of the hill? Young lady, I think you'd better explain yourself."

Melissa started to speak, wondering what lie would serve best, infuriated that Dave was doing whatever it was he was doing. "Well . . ."

Dave pinched her cheek. "Why, she's such a shy little thing. She's got fifteen thousand chickens she's takin' care of. And she's takin' real good care of 'em too. I wouldn't be surprised if she didn't turn out to be about the best grower around this summer."

Evelyn stood up, once again the battleship, although her sails seemed to sag slightly. "My daughter a chicken grower? Never. Melissa, get your things, we're going home."

From the look on Henry's face, Melissa knew he'd swelled to the point he couldn't even speak. Well at least that was something to be grateful for. But the time had come. She either had to go with them or stand up to her mother and say no. She took a deep breath and set fire to the bridge. "I'm not coming just now, Mother."

Evelyn had herded Henry toward the door, never imagining that Melissa wouldn't follow. She turned, and Melissa saw a strange expression cross her face. "I beg your pardon?"

Melissa's voice was soft, but controlled. "I'm not coming. I'll be home in the fall when the chickens are raised. I like it here."

Henry finally found his voice. "If you spend the summer with a...a chicken catcher, just don't bother to come back, Melissa. This is outrageous."

Evelyn hesitated, then regained her authority. "You need therapy, Melissa. I'll arrange it next week. Come, Henry." They started out the door, Lady close on their heels.

Melissa wanted to run to her mother, to try to explain, to make her understand why this summer was so important, but she knew it would be hopeless. She started to follow them, but felt a gentle hand on her arm. She looked up through her tears and saw Dave shake his head slightly. "Let them go, honey."

Melissa stood there, not knowing whether to laugh or cry. Without doubt she'd burned some bridges today and she wasn't used to that. Then she turned her attention back to Dave. He had planned and engineered the whole thing, she realized with a flash of insight—to get rid of them. She turned and stared into his eyes. "Why did you do that?" She needed time to sort things out.

Dave tried to meet her stare and failed. "I thought you might need reinforcements." He tried a smile and a shrug. "Well, they're gone."

She frowned and chewed her lip. The whole scene had been outrageous. She had never seen her mother so at a loss for words. What would the long-term effects be? "But why the chicken catcher bit? They must think you're some kind of a backwoods bumpkin. You shouldn't have done it."

He cupped her chin in his hand and kissed her gently. "And if I were that, would it change how you feel about me?"

Melissa felt the warmth spread. "Of course not, but . . ."

"Would you feel differently if I owned the company rather than if I caught chickens for them?" She slowly shook her head. "But it would make a difference to your mother, wouldn't it?" She nodded. "Melissa, it's what *you* feel that's important, not what anyone else thinks."

She pulled away from him. "I know that, but she's my mother. She must think this is a loony bin."

"Probably. But is it so important what she thinks?"

Melissa picked up the coffee cups and started to the kitchen. "I don't know anymore what's important." Then the thought hit her. "What makes you think I need your help and protection anyway?"

He shrugged. "At least it made the odds even."

"So you just replace my mother or Henry as my guardian, right? I don't want a guardian. I want to manage my own life, Dave."

Dave turned to leave, a strange set to his shoulders. "I'm sorry if I came across that way." He smiled at her. "Actually I thought the whole thing was kind of funny." He started toward the door. "I'll check back later. See how you feel about things."

Melissa followed him to the door and watched him leave, reaching down to stroke Lady. She had to admit Lady hanging on to Henry's pants did give her a new picture of Henry. She was sure she'd never hear from Henry again, and somehow she wasn't even sorry.

She decided that a little sketching might clear her mind. It wasn't even noon yet and Melissa felt as if she'd put in a full day's work in the salt mines. Gathering up her pad and pencils, she chose a spot beside the millpond. As she sketched, she thought how peaceful and pleasant the scene was. But her mind kept going back to the scene with her mother. Dave was right, of course. Her mother was a snob, pure and simple. She would approve a gorilla if he owned the company. After all, look at Henry!

Melissa continued to draw and mull things over. For her part, she much preferred the fact that Dave only worked for the company. That made them kind of equals. If he owned the company, then he would just be another authority figure for her to be appended to. As her thoughts turned to Dave, she thought of the incident this morning while they'd been painting the house. She knew she was becoming very infatuated with the man. She studiously avoided the word *love* in thinking about him. Not that anything would ever come of it, but no one had ever made her feel the way he did, and she liked it.

Melissa finally began the color work, carefully washing paint over the heavy paper, creating a fantasy around the pond. She'd come to the conclusion that this morning had indeed been pretty funny, remembering the expressions on her mother's and Henry's faces when Dave told them she was a very successful chicken grower.

She heard the truck drive in and managed a wave, but could not stop painting at that moment. Melissa was very much aware of Dave as he came to stand behind her. "You're good. Much better at this than painting houses."

"Um." She hunched over the paper, mouth twisted as she added tiny details. She finished the last leaf and sat back to look. "It's not very good. I just don't get enough practice."

"Looks good to me. I think you should do more."

Melissa beamed. Her mother had always considered her art a waste of time. "Do you really think so?"

"Uh-huh. Feeling better about things now?"

She nodded, looking up at him. "I'd like to know where you got that awful accent, though."

He laughed and sat down in the grass. "I grew up with it. It comes in handy from time to time." He reached for her hand. "Dinner with me tonight?"

"Why not? We may have time to eat before the men in the white coats come for me."

He traced the soft inside of her arm with a gentle finger. "What will they do?"

Melissa shrugged. "I wish I knew. I still feel bad about this morning."

"Don't. One day you'll laugh about it." He pulled her down on the grass. "In the meantime we'd better go eat. You have to keep up your strength, you know." He nuzzled her neck and told himself to get up and take her to dinner. "Or we could..."

Melissa unexpectedly had a vision of Dave making love to her right there in the grass. She had to admit the thought wasn't nearly as shocking as it would have been a week ago. "My mother would consider that definitely tacky."

Dave roared with laughter and stood, pulling her up with him. He held her close. "I guess she would at that." He looked her over. "Uh, do you want to think about changing clothes before we leave?"

Melissa realized she was still wearing the paint-spattered clothes. "I thought yellow was one of my better colors."

"Well, it certainly brightens your complexion."

Dave released her and started up the hill. "While you clean up, I'll do your chores." It was better to be doing the chores than sitting in the next room while she was taking a shower. After all, there were limits to a man's control.

Melissa waved and hurried into the house to shower and change, having noted as he walked away that he wore beautifully tailored blue slacks and a pale-ivory knit shirt. They must be going somewhere other than the Dairy Queen, she thought happily. She would put aside her worries about the day and enjoy the evening. Deep down she felt something important was about to happen in her life, that she was going to experience things she'd never even dreamed of, and that Dave would be responsible. She shivered with anticipation, remembering the fire he'd caused in her blood. She just hoped she would know what to do when the time came.

CHAPTER EIGHT

MELISSA'S SPIRITS were high. She'd got through the weekend and half the week with no serious recriminations from the Tulsa contingent. On this particular morning she sat drawing the old house, its age and character coming alive on the pad. She and Dave had gone to the Civil War battlefield park in Prairie Grove on Sunday, and she knew that watercolor scenes in the area were endless. She stared at her subject. The bright morning sunlight hid some of the peeling paint and glinted brightly off the part painted yellow. Melissa knew the yellow would bring new life to the little house. She also knew she had to finish painting it. But the thought of painting the whole house made her tired. Maybe Dave would help again. Or better yet, maybe he knew somebody who painted houses.

Actually, Melissa was somewhat at loose ends on this bright morning. She'd been to check the chickens twice, but they seemed to be doing just fine. She turned her thoughts to Dave. She'd been sure something was going to happen between them, but nothing had. In a way, Melissa was sorry. She was certain now that she was falling in love with Dave, and she was ready to explore that love with him. But while he'd been attentive and seemed to enjoy her company, there had been no more of those soul-searing kisses. She wondered if she had done something wrong.

She put a few more half-hearted strokes on the paper, then stood and decided she'd have to find something else to do besides moon around for the rest of the day. She looked toward Gertie's house and made up her mind. Today would be a great day to rummage through an attic. She walked toward the road, deciding if she found anything, maybe Dave would haul it for her that evening.

The Bates house was a neat white frame structure with a riot of color beginning to show in a variety of old tractor tires and tubs that were scattered around the yard. She followed the driveway around to the backyard, sure she would find Gertie close to the kitchen. The back door opened just as she was about to knock.

"I thought that was you comin' around the house. Come in."

Melissa stepped into the kitchen and sniffed. "Hi. Something sure smells good."

"Fresh apple pie. We'll have some. Have a seat." Gertie waved her to a kitchen chair while she cut the pie.

Melissa looked around her at a dream collection of pie safes, butcher blocks, hall trees and other pieces of oak furniture that would have made any collector drool. "Gertie, where did you get all these wonderful pieces?"

"Pieces of what?"

"This furniture. It's beautiful."

Gertie looked around her. "Oh, this old stuff? Most of it was my momma's. Some was Homer's folks' stuff. A lot of it came out of old barns and farm auctions. Used to be you could buy stuff real cheap at auctions. Here, try this."

Melissa smiled. "You mean before city folks like me started driving the prices up?" Melissa bit into the pie, noticing that Gertie chose to ignore her remark about auctions. "This is incredible. I didn't mean to come over and eat your pie, but I'm glad I did." She took a few more savory bites. "Actually, I wondered if I could take you up on your offer of furniture."

"Been wonderin' why you didn't. You need somethin' to set Pearl's lamp on." Gertie's eyes twinkled. "Finish your pie and we'll take a look."

A short while later, Melissa stood in the middle of the little attic, stooped under the sloping walls, staring and trying to take it all in. Against one wall stood a beautiful old spool bed, its wood dark with age. Scattered through the room was a collection of chairs, chests, tables and various odds and ends. One wall was almost totally covered with old metal tobacco signs. It was a collector's paradise. She watched Gertie rummage in a corner for something. "Gertie, is any of this stuff for sale?"

"Nope. But you're welcome to use any of it you like for as long as you like."

Melissa shook her head. "I can't borrow any of this. What if I break it or something happens to it?"

She saw Gertie look at her in surprise. "Then it's just broke or gone. Be that much I don't have to worry about."

"But someone would love to have these things."

Gertie sat on the edge of the bed. "My kids don't give a hoot nor holler about this stuff." She stroked the wood of the bed. "But I like it. I've gathered it all up over the years and I'd hate to see it go to strangers. I'd like you to use it, honey. Do me good to see it in Pearl's house."

Melissa's heart went out to the woman. She thought of her own mother never saving anything, always wanting the latest new things, then selling or giving away the old. So different from Gertie with her memories scattered throughout this attic. "Well, if you think it's okay."

"I like you. You got spunk and gumption. You'd make a right nice neighbor. Now, what do you want? We'll haul it down the stairs and Homer can bring it over when he comes in for dinner."

Melissa assumed that dinner would be the noontime meal. "Oh, no. I can get it hauled."

"Nope. Get him out of my hair for a spell. Besides, he's been just dyin' to get a look at you, but too proud to go see for himself."

Melissa laughed. These people were unlike any she'd ever known, but she liked them a whole lot. And they treated her like a human being. As she and Gertie struggled down the narrow stairs with the various pieces of furniture, she thought about how nice it was to have real neighbors. She didn't really know her neighbors in Tulsa, and she sure couldn't imagine borrowing furniture from them.

BY MIDAFTERNOON, her new furniture was safely in place and the little house looked like a home for the first time since Melissa had walked in. She'd returned the last of the chicks to the big house and already kind of missed them. She couldn't wait to show Dave. As if by magic, she heard his truck in the drive and felt the now-familiar thrill. She decided to stay in the kitchen so he would have to pass through the new furniture to find her.

She heard the door slam, then a low whistle. She peeked around the kitchen door to watch his progress and admiration. When he finally got to her and kissed her, his face was serious. "What have you been up to today? Rob a furniture store?"

She nodded just as seriously. "I was desperate."

"It's nice." He kissed her again. "Where?"

"Gertie loaned it to me. Homer hauled it over. You should see Gertie's attic."

Dave grinned. "I wondered how Homer was going to get a chance to look you over. It must have made his day. Shall we try it?" He formally handed her into an old sewing rocker and then carefully sat down in what looked to be a handmade, hickory split rocker. "Very nice. Although I kind of liked the boxes and chicks. Gave the place character."

She gave him her best I-choose-to-ignore-that-remark look. "I love it. I just wish she'd sell some of it to me." She watched him rock. "What are you doing off work this early?"

"Oh. I almost forgot why I came by. I was so dazzled by the furniture. I have to run up into Missouri and see some growers tonight, so we'll have to postpone dinner." He rocked a little faster.

Melissa watched him study the arm of his chair. "I didn't know you had growers that far away." Melissa was disappointed, but curious about his work.

"You'd be surprised how far we go. We'll make it up tomorrow, okay?"

"Okay." He almost jumped toward the door and Melissa followed. She thought he was acting a little strangely. "Drive carefully."

He kissed her again and left.

Melissa watched him drive away, wondering why he'd seemed so nervous. She supposed he just felt bad about breaking their date.

Melissa hummed as she fixed supper, scrambling eggs for herself and Lady. She felt sad about the canceled dinner, but thrilled that he'd driven all the way out to tell her instead of just calling. The phone rang and she rushed to answer it, certain it would be Dave, although he had only left two hours before. "Hello."

"Melissa, this is Henry."

Melissa sank to the floor. What a way to ruin a lovely evening! "Yes, Henry."

"You certainly don't sound very glad to hear from me."

"It's late, Henry." An early or a late hour always seemed to be a good excuse for indifference, even if it was neither. Somehow she'd thought Henry would just go away after Saturday and she'd never hear from him again.

"Melissa, I've given a great deal of thought to Saturday."

"Oh?" She braced for the lecture.

"Yes. I'm willing to forgive your little show of theatrics. I assume that chicken catcher is just pushy and you were too polite to get rid of him."

"Oh?" If Henry only knew how pushy!

"Anyway, the monthly meeting for the soybean futures analysts is next Saturday. I'll meet you there at eight in the morning."

Melissa stared at the phone. Forgive her? What had she done wrong—well, at least that Henry knew about? She conjured up a quick mental image of Henry and his soybeans, then a mental image of Dave, muscled, strong, next to her.

"Melissa, they're expecting you. You're one of the hostesses this month."

"Tell them I'm tending chickens and can't make it."

"Melissa, I'm warning you. I have a limited amount of patience."

Angrily, Melissa stood up and clutched the phone. "Henry, you can put your damned soybeans where the sun doesn't shine." She heard her voice and was shocked.

"Melissa!"

"And your analysts, and your hostess duties, and—"

"You're sick, Melissa. You need to see a doctor."

"I'm weller...or whatever...than I've ever been, Henry. Go peddle your soybeans somewhere else." With a grand flourish, she slammed down the phone and stalked into the kitchen, head high, everything else trembling.

"I think I've just burned another bridge, Lady." She toyed with the remains of her meal. "I just wonder what kind of a price we'll pay for our freedom, pretty Lady." She stroked the dog's head. "Whatever it is, let's hope it's worth it."

Melissa gathered up her paints, trying to recapture the happiness she'd felt that morning, knowing it would not be easy. Her thoughts went to Dave. Of all the times for him to leave town! She hoped he would be back soon.

She'd got as far as the porch when the phone rang again. She hurried back in, knowing it would be Dave calling to tell her his trip had been canceled. "Hello." She forced brightness into her voice.

"Well, you certainly sound chipper this evening, considering what you've done." Evelyn Talbut's voice boomed through the receiver.

"Mother." How to ruin one's evening for a second time. Why did they have to call in pairs?

"I just talked to Henry. A heartbroken Henry, I might add."

Henry, heartbroken? That fell in the same category as Henry the stallion. "Mother, I..." Melissa steeled herself. She would not cave in to her mother. Henry's call had already made her angry. She summoned up a new inner strength born of independence and love.

"I must tell you, Melissa, I don't know what's happening to you."

"Maybe I'm growing up, Mother. I..."

"I also want you to know, it wasn't easy to get Dr. Digby off the golf course."

"Who's Dr. Digby?" Her mother seemed to be talking in riddles this evening, not that that was anything unusual.

"Abigail Fletcher's analyst, of course."

Of course. If soybeans had analysts, why not Abigail? "Mother, what are you talking about?"

"He's not taking any new patients, of course, but since Abigail's been in therapy for eighteen years he was willing to make an exception for her dear friend."

"Eighteen years?" You didn't need many patients if you kept them forever.

"These things take time, Melissa. You have an appointment at nine o'clock next Tuesday morning."

"An appointment with who?" Suspicion mushroomed.

"Whom."

"Whom?"

"An appointment with whom, Melissa. Really!"

"That's what I just asked, Mother."

"With Dr. Digby, of course."

"Me? You made me an appointment with a shrink?" Melissa pinched herself. Surely this was all a dream. The conversation sounded like a very campy play from the sixties.

"Therapist, Melissa. Shrink is not a nice word."

"Mother, I am not going to a shrink." Melissa wanted to roll back the clock and not answer the phone the first time. Surely her mother wasn't serious!

"Melissa, I don't know what else to do. You are behaving in a most peculiar manner. I thought it was just a phase, but after your disgraceful behavior toward Henry tonight, I'm convinced you need help. Dr. Digby is very good."

"If he's so good, why hasn't he cured Abigail in eighteen years?"

"Melissa, you've never spoken to me like this."

"Well, you've never told me I'm crazy."

"Not crazy, dear, just misguided."

Melissa took a deep breath, wondering how she could possibly make her mother understand, knowing full well she couldn't. "Mother, I'm not going to the shrink. Henry and I are through. He's a jerk. Please, just let me work things out. I'll be back in the fall."

Melissa heard a wail. "It's that chicken catcher. I knew it."

"He's not a chicken catcher. He—"

"Oh, Melissa, how could you?"

"Mother, he treats me like a real grown-up person, and I...like him very much. Please, Mother, try to understand, I have to do this on my own."

"Oh, Melissa—"

"I'll talk to you later, Mother. And try not to worry. I feel better than I have in a long time." Gently she replaced the phone, feeling saddened. Maybe Dave would be home by ten or so. She hoped he wasn't spending the night in Missouri. She paced the floor. She cleaned the house. At the stroke of ten, she dialed. He answered on the third ring. "Dave?"

"Melissa, what is it?" He sensed the change in her voice.

"Henry called, then Mother."

"Oh, sweetheart, was it bad?"

"Bad enough. I just wondered. Maybe I could come over for a while, get away from here. If it's not too late."

"Over here? To my house?"

"Well, if you're busy." Melissa knew she'd interrupted something. He sounded panicky.

"I'll be right out. We'll go somewhere." There was a pause. "Twenty minutes."

"Okay. Thanks." As Melissa stood staring at the silent phone, the strangeness of his voice really hit her. He hadn't wanted her to come to his house. Why? She poured herself some coffee and started to the porch to wait for him. As she sat down, the thought hit her. Maybe he was married. That would explain it. No, surely not, he would have told her. She wanted to ask him the minute he arrived, but she was afraid to hear the answer.

She sipped the hot coffee, considering this latest possibility. Certainly there were things Dave never discussed, and he did seem closemouthed about his private life, but . . . no, he couldn't possibly be married. Melissa knew deep down that he wouldn't deceive her like that. Dave was one of the few people she'd ever known in her life who was what he seemed.

Melissa pushed the doubts aside. There was plenty of time until the chickens were grown and school started. She would worry about the future then. There was no question in her mind that she would marry Dave in a minute, but it was too soon to think of marriage. For the time being she would content herself with this new world of freedom and love.

CHAPTER NINE

MELISSA'S QUALMS were swept away as soon as Dave stepped out of the truck and headed toward her. As he shuffled a six-pack of Coke Classic and a bag of chips to kiss her, the nagging uncertainty ceased to exist. His kiss started the fires burning at once.

"Mmm, I brought some real Cokes and stuff," he murmured into her ear. "But we can go out if you'd rather. The pizza place is still open."

Melissa drew back and took a deep breath. It was hard to think about food or anything else with him that close. "Well, since you already have everything..." She snatched a Coke and popped the tab. "Umm. This is the closest thing to an addiction I have. It's wonderful." She started into the house, intent on the fizzy drink. Thinking about something besides the kiss, she busied herself in the kitchen.

Dave stood behind her, arms tight around her waist. "Melissa, about coming to my house tonight. It's a disaster area. You know how it is when you live alone." He felt her tense slightly. "Anyway, sometime soon I'll get around to cleaning and..."

"It's okay, Dave, really it is. I just needed to get away from the phone, I guess."

He turned her in his arms. "Then let's get away. Where would you like to go?" His hands stroked her back and his breath was warm against her neck.

Melissa fought the urge to tell him exactly where she would like to go with him. "No, it's okay now." She pressed against him a little tighter, the bowl of chips in her hand forgotten. As his mouth touched hers, she shivered, needing him close, wanting the warm security of his arms. She reached to pull his head down closer and heard his cry. "What is it?"

Dave gingerly removed the bowl from her hand and set it on the counter. "Sharp edges." The rest of the sentence was lost in a kiss. "Are you very hungry?"

"Um . . . I don't think so."

His hands now burned a trail of fire across her back and stomach. "Maybe we could go sit outside." He stepped away from her and retrieved the bowl. When they were sitting on the porch munching chips and sipping the cold Cokes, Dave asked the question that had been lying heavily on his mind. "What did you tell Henry?"

Melissa leaned against him. "I told him where to put his soybeans."

Dave roared with laughter and pulled her closer. "You didn't!"

"I did. Needless to say, he was not amused."

"I guess not. Good for you." He had a mental picture of Henry's reaction to such words from his obedient little Melissa. His voice softened. "And your mother?"

Melissa turned serious. "Would you believe she pulled some shrink off a golf course and set up an appointment for me?" She relayed the conversation. As Dave began to laugh, she punched him. "It's not funny."

He held her wrists. "You may not think so now, but believe me, it's funny. Just picture this guy's golf game being ruined by poor old Abigail and her friend with a tale that the friend's grown daughter has run off with a chicken catcher."

In spite of herself, Melissa began to giggle. "You're awful, you know that?"

He nuzzled her neck. "I know, and you love it. Now, before we get distracted again, tell me all the gruesome details."

Melissa launched into a somewhat exaggerated account of the telephone conversations, stopping only to fetch some dip from the kitchen. As she recounted the conversation about Dr. Digby, she suddenly began to see the humor of it. They giggled like children.

Dave hugged her tight. "See, I told you it was funny."

"Poor Dr. Digby. He may have to cure poor old Abigail just to keep her from referring any more basket cases."

They sat in silence for a moment. "Melissa, are you really happy here?"

She nodded her head vigorously into his shoulder. "I love it here." She wondered if the time had come to mention the fall school term. "I'll miss it." She felt him tense slightly.

His voice was soft. "What about your mother? What will she do now?"

Melissa frowned and crunched another chip. So much for any discussion about school unless she wanted to discuss it with herself. "I don't know. I want her to understand. I know all this must be a terrible shock to her, but I want her to understand and be happy for me. The more I think about it, the more I'm sure she never really liked Henry. She just thought he was a good catch." She turned to him in the dark, a little catch in her voice. "Dave, it's terrible when people think more about money and position and security than about happiness."

He seemed to relax as he pulled her tight again. "I know, sweetheart. But that's the way a lot of people are. You just stay with what you feel and you'll be okay. Your mother would be happy with anyone who could offer you a life she thinks you deserve. Maybe when I get rich and famous..."

She hugged him. "I don't want you rich and famous. I like you just the way you are."

Dave gave her a quick kiss and stood. "Early start tomorrow, honey."

Melissa didn't realize it was so late when Dave left. She could not remember ever being so happy. They had eaten an enormous amount of chips and dip and Melissa realized it had tasted better than all the food in all the fancy restaurants she had ever been to. She had nagging thoughts that it couldn't last, that no one could stay that happy for very long, but she loved it. She began to hope that September would never come.

She cleaned up the chip and dip remains, then retired to her lovely bed and the glow she always felt when Dave was there began to fade. It was late at night, when he was gone, that her misgivings were strongest. She knew he'd changed the subject when she mentioned the fall school term. She didn't want him to feel trapped, just to be honest. If there was no future for them, she could handle that—at least she thought she could. She sighed and snuggled deeper into the soft mattress. Now that the problem with Henry was taken care of, she felt free of guilt—free to get on with her life, and she wanted that life to include Dave. "You're not making sense," she murmured to the quiet room. "You just said you could handle a summer romance, then you say you want him in your future. Why do things have to be so complicated?" A long sigh came from Lady, who was lying beside the bed. Melissa's sigh was every bit as long.

AS THE DAYS PASSED, Melissa knew she was no longer falling in love with Dave. She had arrived. She was as in love with him as any human being could possibly be in love with another. Her painting began to take on a brilliance she'd never thought herself capable of, and she knew it came from the happiness and love she felt.

One Friday afternoon Melissa hurried back from the chicken house, eager to be ready by the time Dave arrived. He was taking her to a bluegrass concert. Melissa had never been to many concerts other than the classical kind and she was excited at the prospect. She was also delighted the chickens were doing so well. They were fully feathered out now and growing by leaps and bounds. The only thing that bothered her about their phenomenal growth was the fact that she was getting closer and closer to the time she would have to make a decision. Soon she would have to let her school know whether or not she would be there for the fall session. She sensed she would not, yet there had been no indication from Dave that he had anything permanent in mind. Slipping into the hot water, she let it wash away her worries along with the dust and grime. She was beginning to feel like Scarlett O'Hara. She would worry about that tomorrow.

She dressed carefully in an off-white eyelet sundress, proud of the tan her farm work had given her. Carefully touching jasmine scent to all the right places she stood back to look at herself. Somehow she looked much more grown-up than she had just a few weeks ago. The little-girl look had been replaced by the unmistakable look of a woman. She had Dave to thank for that. She could also thank him for the rosy glow that seemed to surround her now. Thinking her imagination was running away with itself, she laughed to herself. Her reverie was interrupted by the phone.

Believing it would be Dave, she decided to impart some of the newfound womanhood to her voice.

Adopting what she thought was a sultry posture, she breathed a husky "Hi" into the phone.

The momentary silence was broken with a gasp, followed by the commanding voice of her mother. "My God, Melissa, what's wrong now?"

Melissa's sultry feelings and posture faded immediately. She'd thought the situation with her mother had been resolved last time. Maybe it would never be resolved. "Wrong? Nothing's wrong, Mother." Her voice returned to normal. Squeaky.

"You sounded like Lolita. I suppose you were expecting a call from your precious chicken catcher."

"Mother, he's not a chicken catcher. Not that it makes any difference. What can I do for you?" Melissa was surprised at both the words and the tone of her voice.

"What can you do for me? You can be a good daughter again, for openers. And stop breaking your mother's heart."

"Mother." Melissa took a deep breath and counted to ten. "I am happy. Happier than I have ever been and nothing you can say is going to change that."

"Of course not, but you'll certainly expect me to be around when it's time to pick up the pieces."

"There aren't going to be any pieces, Mother. If there are, I'm perfectly capable of dealing with them myself." Melissa knew the time had come to take a firmer stand. "Mother, it's my life. Please don't try to live it for me." Her voice softened. "Just try to be happy for me."

"Oh, Melissa," her mother wailed. "How could you?" Suddenly the only sound was the dial tone.

Melissa felt bad about the conversation, not to mention the fact that it had ruined her first attempt at sultriness. But she couldn't let her mother interfere with the happiness she felt. And she couldn't very well tell her to put her worries where the sun didn't shine. Saying that to Henry was one thing, but saying it to her mother was a whole different matter. She was glad when Dave arrived. She carefully omitted the conversation from the account of her day.

Melissa looked at Dave in surprise as he pulled into the graveled yard of the little white clapboard school building at Brentwood. Somehow she'd envisioned the arena at the university or at least some bigger building more suitable for a concert. They had instead driven through the mountains to end up at an old schoolhouse in a town that seemed to consist of a grocery store.

Dave looked at her and laughed. "Hardly what you'd expect for a concert, right?"

"Well..."

"Actually it's all amateur talent. Musicians get together here on the weekends to play and sing. But I think you'll like it, even if it isn't the civic center."

They walked in to find the room already jammed with people visiting and musicians tuning up. Everyone seemed to know Dave and he introduced Melissa to countless people whose names she would never be able to remember. She wished now she'd worn something else. Between introductions she whispered in his ear, "Why didn't you tell me so I could have changed clothes?"

He brushed her neck with a kiss. "Because you look absolutely beautiful, that's why. I wanted to show you off."

Melissa felt a moment of discomfort as she sat on the hard wooden chair amidst the audience that ranged from young back-to-the-landers to old-timers. Then the music started.

Melissa's toe began to keep time with the fiddles and the banjos and by the time the first group had relinquished its place to another, she felt as if she'd been coming to the old schoolhouse for ages. She felt a strange kinship to these people and their music, almost as if she'd been there before. Everyone was friendly and treated her as if she were one of them.

At the break, Dave went to get coffee and Melissa looked around her, suddenly overcome by a kind of detachment. She realized that these people were of what her mother would call "a different social class," people Melissa would certainly never have encountered in Tulsa. Yet, they seemed to possess a quality and reality with which she felt comfortable. They were like Gertie, real people. Melissa had a sudden insight that she had somehow come home.

She and Dave sat sipping the hot coffee as he told her about the various musicians and regulars in the audience. "I've been coming here for a lot of years." What he didn't tell her was that here he was Dave, a person, not Dave the businessman. "I don't know which I love best, the people or the music."

She reached up to touch his cheek. "I love all of it." She settled back to listen to the music, her toe tapping with enthusiasm. This was another totally new experience and she soaked it up, eager to see all the different facets of the man she loved.

Dave glanced at her by his side. "I thought maybe you would."

Melissa shivered in the warm night as the music started again. She glanced sideways at Dave, proud that he'd brought her, that he seemed to be showing her off. Catching just a hint of a frown on his face before he turned to her and smiled, she shivered again. Maybe he was sorry he'd brought her. Maybe she didn't fit in. He caught her expression.

"Melissa, what is it?"

"Nothing. I just thought you looked worried."

He reached over to touch her. "Just something that came up at work today. Can't seem to turn it off."

Melissa leaned against him and turned back to the music, her frown and thoughts swept away with the music.

By the time they left the old schoolhouse, Melissa had extracted a promise that they would return the next week. Melissa snuggled against him in the darkness of the car. "That was wonderful, Dave. I had no idea people or places like that even existed."

"That's because you've led a very sheltered life, my dear. It's time we changed all that."

"You're right. How come everybody in the world seems to know you?"

"Because I grew up here. In a rural area, everybody knows everybody else, not to mention everything they do, too."

Melissa sat up straight. "What do they think about us?"

"Probably that we're sleeping together. It's not a bad idea. Does that bother you?"

Melissa was grateful for the darkness as she felt her cheeks redden. "No, that is . . . why would they think that?"

Dave laughed. "That, my love, is one of the mysteries of the world. All I know is that in a rural area, everyone seems to know what everyone else is doing and with whom they are doing it, usually *before* they're doing it."

"Oh, dear."

He pulled her closer. "Don't worry about it. Nobody bothers you or condemns you, they just keep close track, that's all."

Melissa hunched down in the seat. "But I can't stand anyone thinking that. How can I ever face them again?"

"Face them? I'll have you know I'm considered a pretty good catch around here." Hopefully she wouldn't know how good a catch for a while yet. "You should be strutting, not hiding under my arm."

Dave left early that night, pleading another early start, although Melissa wondered what he could have to do on a Saturday. As Melissa lay listening to the night sounds, she wondered again about where he lived. She thought about looking it up in the phone book, but decided against it, not wanting the bubble to burst yet in case she found something she wasn't expecting. He seemed not to want to talk about his job or his private life, and while Melissa thought it strange, she wasn't ready to force the issue. She knew instinctively that he wouldn't deceive her about anything really important. She also knew deep down that her love for him made everything else seem like unimportant details, things they could work out later. She just hoped he felt the same way.

She finally dozed off to dream about her little white-and-yellow farmhouse with Dave there all the time. She saw herself fixing breakfast each morning, then sending Dave off to work. Even in the dream she realized it must be true love because she hated breakfast. She saw herself tending the chickens, then painting whenever and wherever she wanted. They would finish painting the house, Dave would mow the lawn, she would fix wonderful meals. It seemed so real in the dream. It was not just a summer romance, it was forever.

The next morning as she came down the hill from the chicken house, Melissa heard Lady frantically barking. She froze in her tracks when she spotted her mother's car parked in front of the house. She debated whether she should simply go back to the chicken house and hope that her mother would give up and leave. But she knew her mother better than that. She had visions of herself starving to death among the chickens before Evelyn would give up.

She squared her shoulders and marched down to meet the latest assault. Lady had convinced Evelyn that remaining in the car would be the better part of valor until Melissa intervened. She opened the car door. "Mother, whatever are you doing here at this hour?" A quick calculation told her that Evelyn must have been up all night to get here this early. One look at her mother's face indicated that she might indeed have been up all night.

Evelyn got out of the car with her usual dignity, but Melissa sensed a difference somehow. "Melissa, I want to talk to you."

Melissa sighed and began to fortify herself. "Mother, please. I'm doing what I want to do." Much to Melissa's surprise, Evelyn reached out and put a hand on her daughter's cheek. Her eyes seemed to glisten.

"I know, dear. That's what I want to talk to you about. Can we have some coffee?"

Melissa's mind raced as she followed her mother into the house and poured the coffee. She'd never seen this side of her mother and she wasn't at all sure how to deal with this new mother. They sat in the rockers and Melissa searched her mind for something to say. "You must have left Tulsa very early, Mother."

"Melissa, I'm here to apologize to you." She held a hand up to silence Melissa's protest. "No, just listen to me." She took a long drink of hot coffee and looked appraisingly at her daughter.

"I have always thought that I did my best for you. In trying to do my best, there are things I didn't tell you. I think the time has come to tell you, then perhaps you can understand why I have acted as I have."

Melissa sipped her coffee, not at all liking the tone of her mother's voice, a tone that indicated dark hidden secrets—secrets Melissa had a feeling she didn't want to know.

"Melissa, your father did not die in Vietnam. At least I suppose he might have, but not while we were married. The last I heard, he was headed for Toledo with his secretary."

Melissa spluttered into the hot coffee. She had always been told that her father died in the war before she was born.

"I know what you're thinking, Melissa, but hear me out. The dates don't jibe for a heroic death, I'm afraid." Evelyn set the cup on the floor and looked out the window, a faraway look in her eyes. "I loved your father desperately. He was my life. We had such wonderful times, and when you were born I thought it a sin to be so happy." She smiled at the memory of that long-ago time and place. "But your father didn't adjust well to family life. A baby seemed to limit his freedom somehow." Her gaze returned to the room and sought Melissa. "Anyway, he left when you were only a few months old."

Melissa's heart went out to this woman who suddenly didn't seem like her mother, but like a stranger who'd been carrying a terrible burden alone all these years. "Why didn't you tell me?"

"Because I wanted to protect you. Thanks to my parents, we never lacked for anything and I was able to provide the best for you." She clutched Melissa's hand, a look of desperation in her eyes. "Don't you understand, Melissa? I didn't want the same thing to happen to you. I didn't want you to fall in love with someone unsuitable and have to suffer as I did. I wanted you to have security and companionship, not a fleeting love that would crush you when he left."

"Mother, I would have understood."

"You were too young. I didn't want you to have bitter feelings about your father, I just wanted you to have the best of everything with none of the pain. How could I have been so foolish?" Evelyn's eyes filled with tears. "I wanted you to have security, Melissa."

Understanding flashed through Melissa's mind. "Henry."

Evelyn nodded. "Yes, Henry."

Melissa rose and hugged her mother, clinging to her. "But Henry is such a jerk, Mother."

Through the tears, Evelyn spoke. "Yes, but he's a jerk with a very secure future."

Melissa looked at her mother and started laughing. Soon Evelyn joined in at the absurdity of her last statement. "Oh, Melissa, he really is a jerk. You would have been terribly unhappy."

"I know. I finally realized that."

Evelyn wiped her eyes and struggled to her feet. "Now that I've confessed that seedy side of my life, I have something else to say to you. I would not have wished for you to fall in love with this chicken catcher or whatever he is. But you seem to have done so. I hope it works out for you and he doesn't bring you any suffering." She took a deep breath, more her old self now. "At any rate, it is your life to live and I hope you will be happy, whatever you decide."

Melissa threw herself into her mother's arms, something she had not done for many years. "Oh, Mother, I do love him, and so will you when you get to know him. And thank you. I love you."

Evelyn extricated herself, reverting quickly to the familiar battleship. "Really, Melissa, there's no reason to become maudlin. Tell that young man he will have me to deal with if he brings you any unhappiness."

Both women felt more comfortable now that the familiar roles had been resumed. Melissa realized what it had cost her mother to come to her and bare her soul. "I'll tell him. Can you stay for lunch? You could get better acquainted with him then."

"Certainly not. I have a bridge tournament this afternoon." Melissa understood that her mother had to leave, needed to be alone to recover from what she must see as a humiliating experience. "By the way, this place looks much better with furniture. Another auction?"

"No more auctions for me. Ever." Melissa knew that the next time she saw her mother, she would tell her the whole story about the farm. But she decided one earth-shattering revelation a day was enough. "Goodbye, Mother, and thanks for everything."

"Just remember what I told you." As Melissa watched her mother get into the car she thought she saw her bite her lip, and caught the sunlight reflecting in the glistening eyes.

Melissa watched the car disappear from view, seeing her mother not as the overwhelming figure of authority she had known all her life, but as a young frightened mother, abandoned by the man she loved, struggling to raise her daughter as best she could. From now on she would see that image of her mother and she would understand. She'd never felt this close to her mother. As she turned toward the house, she suddenly let out a squeal of delight. Her mother approved of Dave—well, maybe not approved, but at least was willing to entertain the possibility. She must tell Dave.

She tapped the floor impatiently as the phone continued to ring on his private number. When he finally answered, she launched into a rapid explanation. "Dave, I have wonderful news. We have to celebrate. My father wasn't a war hero, he deserted us."

There was a slight pause. "Well, that certainly sounds like good news to me."

Melissa ignored the cautious tone. "But don't you see what it means? He ran off to Toledo with his secretary. That's why we have to celebrate."

Again the cautious voice. "That certainly sounds like a reason to celebrate." Another pause. "Melissa, what the hell are you talking about?"

"My mother. She was here. Everything's okay now."

"Whatever you say. Now calm down and tell me what happened."

Melissa reported the conversation to him, ending with her mother's qualified expression of approval of her "chicken catcher."

Dave finally laughed. "That's great, sweetheart. I'm glad she came. Her stock just went up in my book. By the way, you have a date for dinner tonight. A real celebration: dinner, drinks, the works."

His voice had taken on a silky, seductive tone, and there was no doubt in Melissa's mind that part of that celebration would include . . . well, something very exciting. She shivered at the tone of his voice. "I'll be waiting." She hung up the phone and whirled around the room, happy beyond words. Evelyn's blessing, while not necessary, was icing on top of the cake. She headed for the bedroom to prepare for the upcoming celebration, then realized it was not even noon. What on earth would she do to occupy herself for the whole day? She grabbed the broom. When in doubt, clean house.

CHAPTER TEN

DAVE AND MELISSA SAT at a small table in the corner
of the Ribhouse in nearby Fayetteville, waiting for
their meal. Dave absentmindedly smoothed the red-
checkered tablecloth and looked at the woman across
the table. The dark-green blouse seemed to make her
eyes glow and her hair burn. "I hope you like ribs."
He knew it was a stupid thing to say, but if he said
what he was thinking, they'd be thrown out of the
place.

She sipped at her beer. "Well . . ."

"You've never eaten ribs. Mother thinks they're
low-class."

Melissa shook her head. "Everyone's eaten ribs,
Dave. I've just never made a study of them, that's
all."

Dave swallowed his laughter with the beer. "Well, I
have. And this place serves some of the best." At that
moment, the waitress slapped down a platter of
steaming ribs and a basket of garlic bread. "Dig in."

Melissa had always been taught to eat everything
with knife and fork, but the sight of Dave attacking a
rib with fingers and teeth made her feel reckless. After all, when in Rome and all that. She picked up one

of the succulent ribs and tentatively bit into it. The flavor was totally unexpected and suddenly she was starving. She attacked the rib with enthusiasm.

Dave watched her, seeing her nod with approval. Like all hungry people, they ate with little conversation, happy with each other and the excellent food.

The longer Melissa ate, the messier she became. She had sauce all over her hands and mouth. She put down her rib to wipe her hands, licking the corners of her mouth before she applied the napkin there. As she looked up, she caught Dave staring at her mouth. He seemed frozen in motion, a rib halfway to his mouth, desire flickering in his eyes. She smiled and licked her upper lip. His expression didn't change. Suddenly, she frowned. "What are you staring at?"

"Oh...nothing." He reached over and wiped her chin with his napkin. After all, there were limits. "Good?"

"Delicious. They're a lot better when you eat them with your fingers." She attacked the rib again.

Dave smiled weakly. He had to think about something besides those soft lips and beautiful white teeth. "Have you had any formal instruction in painting?" That seemed a safe subject.

Melissa shook her head, licked her lips and answered, curious about his choice of topics. "No. I just always liked to draw things. I got some books on watercolors and started." She sipped her beer. "This is a real celebration tonight."

"I know." He squeezed her hand. "I'm really proud of you."

She stopped to lick her fingers and heard Dave groan. "Are you okay? You're not sick or anything?"

"No. You were saying?"

"Oh. Well, I just feel different tonight. Maybe it's because everything seems to be going in the right direction now. Saying no to Mother was the best thing I've ever done. I guess it made her think or something. Anyway, I feel closer to her than I ever have. And it would never have happened if I hadn't said no."

"I'm glad you did, Melissa. People should allow other people to live their own lives."

"I agree. Let's drink to people living their own lives." She drank from the mug. "I'm just glad Mother understands now."

"So am I. You know, it took a lot for her to tell you the truth after all these years." Dave watched her beam, then turned his attention to the check. "Ready?"

She nodded and stood up, brushing crumbs from the white linen sundress. "That was a wonderful dinner, Dave. Thank you." She leaned over and kissed his cheek, noticing his eyes were now unreadable.

Dave caught the mixed scent of jasmine and hickory smoke and thought it should be bottled. "You're welcome."

On the ride home, she sat close to him. Dave concentrated hard on driving, almost flinching every time she touched him, but Melissa seemed too happy to notice.

Lady greeted them as if they'd been gone for days. "Think we'd abandoned you, pretty girl?" Melissa stooped to pet the dog. "It's such a beautiful night." Her eyes scanned the starry sky. "I'll make coffee and we can drink it by the pond."

"Great. I'll get the quilt." Dave retrieved the quilt from his truck and spread it on the bank, thinking the water was nice and close in case he needed to jump in.

Melissa returned quickly with two steaming mugs. They sat on the old quilt, sipping coffee and listening to the night sounds. Dave's fingers traced an intricate pattern down Melissa's arm and he felt her shiver, then relax. He finished his coffee and retraced the pattern with his lips.

Melissa quivered with excitement. She sensed something important might happen tonight, and knew that she was ready. As Dave's warm lips moved along her arm, the fire began to burn deep within. She touched his cheek with a shaky finger. She wanted to touch him, to know all of him, but she was afraid. Henry had always insisted that she should not allow herself to be carried away by physical feelings. He'd said it was unbecoming. And the things she instinctively felt tonight would definitely be unbecoming. She didn't want Dave to think her forward.

Dave felt the light touch and suspected the reason. "I want you to touch me, Melissa." He pulled her down and gently touched her lips with his. "Do whatever feels right, sweetheart." He felt her inexperienced touch on his neck. Surely she wasn't... His kiss deepened as he searched for evidence she'd walked this road before.

Melissa opened her lips to him, feeling heat radiate through her body. She ached where no ache had ever been. She touched his back, felt the powerful muscles. She wanted her skin against his. She whispered in his ear, her breath scorching his very skin. "Dave, I'm not very good at this."

Dave took a deep breath. "Honey, if you were any better, I'd kill myself. Just do what you feel like doing."

"What I mean is..."

He placed a finger over her lips. Maybe she was still... He pulled back. Knowing Henry, it was certainly possible. He had to think before going any further. "Why don't we take a swim?"

"Now?"

He nodded and stood up, peeling off his shirt. "Why not?"

"I don't have a suit." Melissa felt abandoned and upset. What had she done wrong to make him suddenly leave her and want to swim? She wanted to love this man, not go swimming.

"Neither do I. But I have some very stylish designer briefs." He stood on one leg and pulled off one shoe. At least a dip in the cold water would cool him down; then, perhaps, he could think rationally. "Your underwear will do just fine. After all, it's dark."

Melissa considered the situation. She'd never been swimming at night or in just her underwear. Maybe it was time she tried both. She couldn't imagine why they were doing this, but why not? She unhooked the back of the sundress.

Dave stood at the edge of the water, clad only in his briefs. He watched her reach behind her back. In the pale moonlight, he saw the sundress fall to her feet. Her creamy skin seemed to reflect the silver light. He raced into the water, hoping it wouldn't steam when he hit it. He surfaced to find her wading in, water lapping at her thighs.

She saw him stare at her for a moment, then fly into the water. She waded toward him.

"This is fun! It's not even cold." She lay down in the water, floating toward him. She splashed water at Dave and he splashed back. They began to frolic like children. Melissa felt the excitement and heat even in the water and reached out to splash him again, but he caught her arm, pulling her through the water toward him. She put her arms around his neck and felt him pull her body against his. She felt their wet bodies melt together and wondered how she could feel so hot immersed in cold water. He wrapped her legs around his waist. She felt the heat concentrate where her thighs touched his hard waist.

His mouth covered hers and he pulled her closer. "Melissa, you're driving me crazy."

"I am?" Melissa liked that very much. She nibbled at his ear, and as some profound memory surfaced in her brain, she began to stroke his shoulders with sure hands. She felt him stand up in the water and head for the bank, still carrying her. She shivered as the night air caressed her wet skin.

"Cold?" At her shake of the head, he gently lowered her to the quilt. "If you are, we could go in the house."

"I love you, Dave." Her voice was tiny. She'd never said those words before. But her body was on fire, throbbing and aching for him. She kissed the drops of water from his face and heard him groan. Her hands touched his hair, his face, the hard muscles across his stomach.

He pulled her close, kissed her, then stopped to wrap the quilt around her shoulders. They sat, the quilt drying them. Melissa wanted more, but was content at that moment. She followed Dave's finger and caught the silver tail of a shooting star. She shivered at the beauty of the night.

OVER MORNING COFFEE, Melissa regretted she hadn't cried out her love for him, but she had stopped short of it. She'd feared that would frighten him, that he would not come back. He'd said nothing about love, after all. But surely, after last night— She bit back the words, content to love and see what happened. She walked to the end of the drive and waved him good-bye, waving to Gertie at the same time. The older woman was tending the many flowers in her yard and had straightened to watch Dave drive away. Melissa watched Gertie wave at the truck and wondered if she knew Dave. She'd have to ask her.

Melissa hummed as she fixed breakfast for herself and Lady. Melissa didn't eat in the morning as a rule, but she felt starved on this occasion.

She waltzed through her morning chores, feeling as if she were three feet off the ground. Even the chickens were beautiful this morning. She'd never felt so wonderful. A day had never been so beautiful. She thought she would like to paint again, sure that the beauty of her feelings would show in her work. She couldn't wait to get her paints out. But first, the chickens.

Melissa stood at the end of the chicken house and looked out over the sea of white chickens. They filled every square inch of the house now. It was hard to believe that only four weeks ago the little yellow biddies had seemed lost in the huge house. But the biddies had rapidly become big chickens, sleek and white with bright red combs. She leaned against the wall and watched them eat and drink, realizing, and admitting for the first time that they were almost ready to go to the processing plant.

Although Melissa did not feel the same attachment to the grown chickens that she had felt for them as baby chicks, she still felt a pang of regret and more than a little sadness over the fate of the birds she had worked so hard to raise. She knew now what Gertie had meant that day. And she knew she wasn't cut out to raise chickens, knowing each batch would be in her care only a few weeks.

As she continued to watch the chickens, unmindful of the heat in the house, her mind moved on. The size of the chickens meant the summer was almost over and she was rapidly running out of time to make her decision.

She and Lady walked slowly back down the hill, enjoying the warm summer morning, knowing the comfortable warmth would turn to uncomfortable heat before the day ended. Much as her fingers itched to paint, she realized it was already too hot. She would have to wait until evening. She wondered idly what she should do to fill the hours until evening when Dave got off work.

She gave the house a quick once-over and settled down with a glass of tea. She wished Dave would give her some sort of indication about the future. She supposed she could bring it up, but... She was much more independent now than when the summer began, but not *that* independent. Her thoughts were interrupted by the phone. "Hello?"

"Melissa?" The voice seemed unsure of itself. Melissa wondered briefly if she'd forgotten to pay the electric bill or something. She certainly didn't recognize the voice.

"Yes?"

"Oh, good. You're certainly not the easiest person to find. I finally got your number from your mother."

"Oh?" Melissa still had no idea who this person was, but certainly wished she would identify herself.

"This is Sally from Mr. Williams's office."

Melissa sank into a chair. Mr. Williams was her principal. "I didn't recognize your voice. What can I do for you?" Melissa knew exactly what Sally wanted, but she might as well hear it.

"Well, we hadn't heard from you." A pause. "Mr. Williams just wanted to make sure everything's set for school. It won't be long, you know."

Melissa thought that might be the understatement of the century. She gathered from Sally's tone that they must have gotten wind of her breakup with Henry. It was hard to tell what else they'd heard. "I've just been too busy. The summer's just raced by."

"Shall I tell him you'll come by in the next week or so to sign your contract?"

Melissa sighed. The moment of truth was at hand. However, perhaps it could be delayed a bit. "Tell him I'll talk to him very soon."

This time there was a long pause. "You are going to teach this fall, aren't you?"

The questions were getting more direct and more difficult to evade. "As far as I know, yes. But tell him I'll let him know for sure within the week. And thanks for calling." She quickly hung up before Sally could demand any explanations.

Resuming her position and taking another sip of tea, she knew something had to happen soon. She was certain Dave felt the same about her as she did about him—at least she was pretty sure he did. So why couldn't he just come out and say it and they could get married? Then she wouldn't have to go back to Tulsa. Of course, if he were already married, that would certainly explain why he didn't do it, but she couldn't believe that. Maybe he lived in some awful place that he was ashamed of. Or maybe he really was a chicken catcher and he was ashamed of that. Well, she didn't care what he was. She loved him and that was all that mattered.

She would mention the call from the school tonight and see what he had to say. Maybe she would just propose to him. After all, everyone was liberated these days. Melissa decided she would convince Dave tonight that whatever his situation, it was nothing to be ashamed of, and then she would simply tell him they had to decide something before next week. Feeling a lot better, Melissa gathered up her paints and headed for the secluded little spot by the pond. She would ignore the heat and paint anyway.

Melissa sat in the shade of the willows and looked out at the millpond, smooth and glassy in the summer heat. She had talked at length with Gertie about the old mill that had sat beside the pond many years ago, and she knew that one day she would try to paint it. Now as she stared at the shimmering surface, the old building, long gone, seemed to float before her eyes. Time seemed to slide back until she could almost see the clapboard building with its huge wooden wheel creaking round and round in the millrace. Her hands seemed to fly.

Melissa finally stopped to brush the damp hair out of her face and look at the painting. She sensed she was not alone and whirled around to find Dave staring at the paper. "My God, Melissa, that's incredible. How did you know?"

Flushing at his presence, she looked from him back to the paper. "Gertie told me what it looked like. Why?"

Dave continued to stare. "It burned when I was just a little kid, but I remember it. It was a relic then, but that's what it looked like."

Melissa smiled, pleased with his reaction. "Do you like it?"

He shook himself, then looked at Melissa. "I like it very much. You are a very talented artist, you know that?"

"Not really, but I love trying."

He pulled her from the chair and drew her close. "No, Melissa. You're good. You should be doing this full-time." His mouth found hers, gentle, yet demanding. "Well, almost full-time."

Melissa basked in his praise. As his kisses deepened, she felt the familiar fire begin to burn deep within her. She marveled that after so many weeks, her love for this man continued to grow. Her hands sought the strong back muscles under his shirt. "Mmm...I'm glad you approve."

He pulled her tight and kissed her with the urgency she knew so well. "Sweetheart, unless you want to be thrown down and ravished right here in broad daylight, you'd best stop now."

She laughed and nibbled his earlobe. "You wouldn't."

"Oh, but I would." His fingers traced a line down her collarbone to her halter.

Melissa pulled back and laughed. One look in his eyes showed the depth of his desire and suddenly Melissa had no doubt that he just might carry out his threat. She quickly pulled away and began gathering up her things.

He gave her an affectionate pat and picked up her paints. "No sense of adventure, I see. Must not play with fire unless you're ready to get burned, my dear." He gave her a quick kiss. "And I am burning right now." He laughed and watched Melissa hurry toward the house.

Melissa set the painting of the mill on the old-fashioned mantel and stood back to admire it. She was very pleased with her effort. "It really isn't bad, is it?"

Dave stood behind her. "No, it really isn't. Now, what would you like to do about dinner?"

Melissa felt Dave's chest rub against her back. She knew what she would like to do about dinner. "I'd better go check the chickens first."

"You are a master at changing the subject, did you know that?" Hand in hand they walked up the hill as Lady darted ahead of them.

After a quick check, they stood for a moment where Melissa had stood that morning. Dave's voice seemed quiet. "You've done a fantastic job with them. They'll be ready to go in a week or two." His voice seemed to hold a trace of the sadness she had felt that morning.

Melissa decided this was as good an opening as she was likely to get. "My school called this morning." She saw and felt him tense.

"And?"

"They just wanted to know if I was going to sign my contract." It seemed to Melissa that even the chickens had stopped to listen.

Dave took a deep breath and continued looking at the chickens. "What did you tell them?" He held his breath waiting for her answer.

Melissa shrugged. "I told them I'd let them know in a few days." They were on very sensitive ground right now and Melissa wanted to hear his response. When none was forthcoming, she continued. "I have to decide." She watched Dave walk over to a water pipe and adjust something she knew didn't need adjusting. Panic struck and for a moment, she thought he was just going to keep walking, out of the chicken house, out of her life. His back was still turned when he spoke.

"What do you *want* to do?"

Melissa wanted to grab him and tell him that she loved him and didn't ever want to go back, that she wanted to stay with him forever, but the words wouldn't come. "I haven't decided yet. I might just stay here." She looked at the strong back, the wide shoulders. They visibly seemed to relax.

"Well, you could do fine raising chickens." He turned toward her, but his eyes were shaded by his cap.

Melissa felt worse than she had after talking to the school that morning. Somehow the conversation wasn't going exactly as she'd wanted it to, it wasn't even close. "I feel like junk food tonight." She hoped her declaration sounded bright as she turned to leave the chickens. She tried desperately to keep the disappointment out of her voice and straightened her shoulders, afraid to look in his face. She'd been so sure he would ask her to stay.

He walked to her and put an arm around her waist. "Junk food it is."

An hour later, they sat in a corner booth eating fat hamburgers, real French fries, and sipping draft beer. "Melissa, I would love for you to stay, but it's a decision you have to make. You have to do what you want to do."

She wiped her mouth, thinking how trite that sounded. All her life she'd wanted someone to tell her to do what she wanted, but suddenly she didn't want to hear it from Dave. She wanted him to say something else. "I know, but I'll worry about it tomorrow." Maybe he didn't love her as much as she loved him. Maybe it was just a summer romance for him. On the other hand, she'd never really told him she loved him either—not really told him properly, whatever the proper way might be. The evening just wasn't going right. She took a hefty swig of beer. She couldn't believe she'd been so happy with this man for weeks and suddenly felt so strained in his presence. She emptied the mug.

When they finally got home, Melissa wasn't sure whether to demand that he make love to her all night, or to demand that he leave so that she could drown herself in the millpond. Why did things have to be so complicated? The decision was taken from her when he kissed her good-night and left. Well, she could always drown herself another day.

MELISSA BOUNCED down the hill from the chicken houses the next morning to find Gertie waiting on the porch. "Hi, Gertie! I've been meaning to come see you. I don't know where the time goes."

The woman grinned. "I just thought I better check in on you. I knew you'd been plenty busy." Her eyes twinkled. "You must be real special for Dave himself to check on your chickens. I been seein' that truck here a lot, but I didn't know till yesterday it was Davey."

Melissa wondered what she meant. "He's my field man. You know him?"

"Oh, honey. I've known that boy since he was just a tad of a thing. He's a good boy. Took right over when his daddy died like he'd been runnin' things all his life.''

Melissa felt her stomach turn to stone. She tried to keep her voice light. ''Well, I guess he's done okay for himself.''

The woman looked closely at Melissa, seeming to sense that something was wrong, that Melissa really thought Dave Winston was a field man. ''Anyway, did you hear about the wreck last night out on the highway?''

Melissa knew Gertie was trying to change the subject, but she had to know. Now. ''Gertie, just what is his position in the poultry company?''

''Oh, Melissa, honey, I seem to have put my foot in it again.''

''I want to know.'' The lump that was her stomach seemed to grow and grow.

''Honey,'' she said in a soft voice, ''he owns the company.''

CHAPTER ELEVEN

MELISSA SAT ALONE in the house, wondering what to do. Gertie had gone to great lengths to try to convince her that if Dave didn't want to tell her he owned the company, he must have a good reason for it. But Melissa could only believe he hadn't told her because he was amusing himself for the summer at her expense. A new toy, a naive little city girl who'd made a mess of things. Anger and hurt welled within her. She felt used. Staring at the phone, she decided the best thing would be to get it over with. She dialed. "Mr. Winston, please."

A competent voice replied, "I'm sorry, he's out for the day. May I take a message?"

"No. No message." Melissa looked at the painting of the day before with a sadness that threatened to engulf her. Shaking herself, she knew she couldn't mope around all day, she must stay busy. He would be there that evening, and they could hash it out.

The day dragged as Melissa played her mother's story over and over in her mind. She was sure she had tried to be objective, but try as she might, she had been unable to come up with any good reason for his deception. Time was not her friend now. She'd had all day to think about it and there just wasn't any reasonable explanation for his behavior—except that he'd used her. By late afternoon, her hurt had grown to a raw aching wound.

When she heard the truck enter the driveway, she walked slowly to the door, determined not to make a scene, determined to retain what dignity she could—determined to let him try to explain. More than anything she wanted to hear a simple explanation. But when she saw his smiling face, her anger welled again. "Why didn't you tell me?" she demanded.

The smile vanished and he opened the door. "Melissa, what is it?" But he knew. He knew from the look on her face.

"Why? You're no different from the rest of them. Take care of stupid little Melissa. She obviously can't take care of herself. Use her, order her around, do whatever strikes your fancy. You lied to me. I suppose you have a wife and six kids who wouldn't approve of your activities." Melissa felt all the hurt and anger coming out. "How could you? You treated Lady better than you treated me." She turned to run toward the back door, but he grabbed her arm.

"You're going to listen to me, whether you want to or not. Sit." He led her to one of the rockers, then slouched into the other. "Melissa, I know I was wrong. God, don't you think I know it? Don't you think I've lain awake nights wondering how to tell you?"

"About the wife or about the company? I'm not a child. You could have just told me."

He tried to take her hand, but she pulled back. "Melissa, there is no wife. No kids. I'm not that big a heel. At first, I was afraid. I was afraid you were like the others, just after the money. I didn't want the money to interfere."

"Thanks a lot."

"Honey, of course you're not, but by the time I knew that, I'd fallen in love with you. Then I didn't know how to tell you. I love you, Melissa, but I could see that people had been ordering you around all your life, that you wanted an equal, not another authority figure. And money and position sometimes spell authority. I was afraid I'd lose you."

She stared at him, wanting to believe him, but too hurt to keep the tide of feelings inside. "You deceived me. You used me, knowing I'd go away in the fall. You certainly didn't have anything earth-shattering to say when I told you I had to make a decision about teaching."

He started to reach for her hand again. His face showed the pain he felt. "Oh, Melissa, I wanted to tell you to forget teaching forever. I wanted to. But if you'd known who I was, you'd have run back to that school, afraid I would just be the next phase in your well-planned existence. I wanted you to want to stay here with me, then I would have told you. But I wanted that decision to be yours. Obviously it was faulty reasoning on my part." He leaned toward her.

"I want to marry you, but I can't make the decision for you. I wanted you to want to stay here because you loved me and wanted to be here, not because I was pressuring you to marry me."

"So now, all of a sudden, you want to marry me? I may be naive, but I'm not stupid. Why would you just happen to come up with that idea after I found out?" Could he really be telling the truth?

"I wanted to ask, but I had to think of a way to tell you about the company. I've really screwed things up, haven't I? Melissa, I do love you."

"Sure. So I trade Henry and Mother for some other big shot who can take over my care and feeding. Big deal." Melissa wanted to take it back before it was out of her mouth, but she couldn't. She was like a hurt animal, striking out at the person trying to help.

The blue eyes flashed. "That's not fair and you know it!"

She did know it, but she couldn't take it back. She had to have time to think, time to sort it all out. And she couldn't do that with the man she loved sitting so near. "I'll finish raising the chickens, then I'll go back where I belong. I think you'd better leave."

He stood and reached to touch her, then didn't. "I do love you, more than I've ever thought it possible to love anyone. I know I've hurt you, but don't shut me out. Think about it." He moved to leave, the fine strong body just a little slumped. "You know where to find me."

Melissa watched him leave, tears coursing down her cheeks. She had to hold on to the door to keep herself from running after him. Maybe he'd been telling the truth. Maybe he did want to marry her. But suddenly she didn't feel as if she knew him. He wasn't a workingman. He wasn't her equal anymore. He was a wealthy powerful man. How could her whole world change overnight?

MELISSA HAD WORKED out a routine to stay busy so she wouldn't have time to think about Dave so much. She had concluded that she loved him desperately, but couldn't think of a way to take back the harsh things she'd said. She had even begun to believe that he'd told her the truth, but as each day passed without any message from him, she was less sure. She'd been sure he'd call.

"Lady, maybe we should just stay here. What do you think?" She talked to the dog almost constantly now, unsure why, maybe taking comfort from the sound of her own voice. They walked down the hill from the chicken houses, Melissa forcing herself to enjoy the late summer afternoon, Lady foraging for rabbits in the tall grass. "Maybe I'll go talk to my friendly banker tomorrow." Melissa knew Mr. Felker would be overjoyed to see her again. But she had to do something. The chickens would go in another week. If she could lease the poultry operation and get a job doing something, she and Lady could stay. But even as she said it, she knew it was wishful thinking. She knew she would have to go back to Tulsa and teach. It was where she belonged. Her decision made, she went to the phone. "Gertie? Melissa."

"Oh, Melissa, I've been worried sick about you. I could just kick myself for tellin' you what I did."

Melissa didn't want to get into lengthy explanations with anyone. "No, you did the right thing. Listen, could Homer do me a favor?"

"Sure, honey, you just name it."

"I've got to drive to Tulsa tomorrow. I'll check the chickens in the morning and I should be back by early afternoon. I just wondered if Homer could check them at noon?"

There was a long pause. "Course he can. I hope you're not goin' back."

Melissa tried the light touch. "Well, after all, it's almost time to start school. My school sent out a search party last week."

"Honey, it ain't none of my business, but when you get old, meddlin' comes as a right. I don't know why Davey did what he did, but I do know he's a good boy. He had a bad time with one wife, and he might have been gun-shy. But if you'd talk to him..."

"Gertie, I just... I don't know. Maybe in time."

"If you're goin' back to Tulsa, don't seem to me like you got time. Talk to him, child. I'd bet he's hurtin' just as bad as you are. And that's all I got to say on the subject. Homer'll see to your chickens tomorrow."

"Thanks, Gertie." She wondered how Gertie could possibly know how seriously the breakup had affected her. As she sat on the porch, she remembered the bluegrass concert and Dave's remark about rural people knowing what was going on. Likely, Gertie had known how serious it was the day she'd spilled the beans. Melissa had obviously taken the news with all the coolness of someone off to the firing squad. Maybe Gertie was right, she should just call him. No, she would go to Tulsa tomorrow, start setting her life in order again.

MELISSA STARTED for Tulsa early the next morning. Traffic was light so she made good time. When the city came into view, she was glad to see it. Kind of glad to see it. But she kept thinking about her little house and Viney Grove as she fought the early morning traffic in the heart of the city. But she was doing what she had to do.

As she walked into her school, she was overcome with mixed emotions. She liked teaching, but there was not the excitement she usually felt. She encountered Mr. Williams as she walked into the office.

"Well, Melissa, we were beginning to think you'd fallen off the face of the earth. Have a good summer?"

She nodded, glancing around at all the familiar sights of the school. "An interesting summer."

"Well, that's fine. Let me get your contract."

Melissa sat on the edge of the chair as he rummaged through the files. "Sally's not here today, so bear with me. Ah, here it is." He handed the papers to Melissa.

Melissa looked at the contract and knew it was not what she wanted. She wasn't sure how she knew, but something clicked in her mind. "Mr. Williams, I don't think I'm going to be able to teach this year."

The principal looked as if she'd slapped him. "Melissa, is something wrong?"

"No, I'm moving to Arkansas."

"Well, this is rather short notice."

"I know, and I'm sorry. But I'm sure you have plenty of qualified people on the waiting list. I enjoyed teaching here and I'm sorry if I have caused you any trouble." Before he could speak, she rushed out of the building to her car, still not able to believe what she'd just done.

Melissa had plenty of time to think on her way back to the farm. She couldn't believe she'd actually done it. But when she'd looked at the contract, she'd known that she was a different Melissa from the one who'd signed it the year before. The farm was where she belonged. Although at times the memories of Dave threatened to crush her, she knew in time they would mellow and she would remember only the good things. And because of that, she knew she couldn't bear to leave her little house. Perhaps she would never have the man she loved, but she would keep the memories.

She stopped by the bank on the way home and picked up a paper at the grocery. She had a lot of work to do.

Melissa took a deep breath and dialed her mother's number a few days later. It would take all her acting skill to carry it off. "Mother?"

"Melissa, when are you coming home? The school has called again."

"I know, Mother." This was where it got sticky. "I've made arrangements with the school to take a year's leave." There was no reason to tell her mother she'd just out-and-out quit; plenty of time for that later. "I'm staying here for a while." Silence. "It's okay. I got a job with one of the preschools in Fayetteville. And Mr. Felker, the banker, found someone to lease the chicken houses for a year with an option to buy them. I just talked to him today." More silence. "So everything's taken care of." Melissa sighed, wondering if she'd brought it off.

"Melissa, is something wrong?"

"What could possibly be wrong?" She should have known it wouldn't be so easy to fool her mother.

"With that young man?"

"No, Mother, nothing's wrong. I just told you, everything's fine."

"Very well." There was a long pause. "But I'm here if you need me, Melissa."

"Thank you, Mother." Melissa replaced the phone, tears welling in her eyes. Her mother had known something was wrong. But how could she burden her mother with the knowledge that her daughter was treading the same path Evelyn had trod so many years ago? She couldn't. Besides, Melissa didn't want to admit to anyone just yet how badly she'd screwed up. Deep down, she remained sure Dave would call. The pain, held at bay while she was busy with the bank and finding a new job, flooded back, and she wondered if maybe coming back had been a terrible mistake.

THE HUGE TRUCKS LUMBERED into the yard just after dark and Melissa brightened when she saw the familiar white pickup truck following. She hurried to the door just in time to see a total stranger get out of the truck and start toward the door. She realized all the field men drove the white trucks.

"Mizz Talbut? We're gonna pick up your chickens tonight, so don't mind all the racket."

Melissa nodded.

"You might want to watch. It's quite an operation."

Melissa had thought she might want to watch until she looked at the white plastic crates stacked ten high on the trucks. She didn't want to see her chickens chased down and unceremoniously dumped into those crates to be hauled away to slaughter. Not now. She shook her head and muttered some excuse, then watched as the trucks groaned and lumbered their way up the steep hill to the chicken houses. She turned back to the house, tears sliding down her cheeks. She sat on the porch and held Lady tight. First Dave, now the chickens. "You're the only one who hasn't abandoned me, Lady." Her companion silently licked her tears dry and whimpered as if to comfort her.

Melissa lay awake far into the night, listening to the noise coming from the top of the hill, wondering if she should call Dave. He'd said call him, but she was sure he must feel differently about her after all those awful accusations she'd leveled at him. Why hadn't she just listened to his story? But no, she'd had to attack. Maybe when she got settled in her new job. He needed more time, time would heal everything. Wasn't that what the song or poem or whatever it was had said?

MELISSA LAY IN BED watching the morning sun disrupt her darkened cocoon and her sleep. She thought she should get up, but there was really no reason. Though the chickens had been gone for three days, still she woke at dawn. It would be a nice time of the day to paint, but she discovered she wasn't even interested in that now.

She finally dragged herself out of bed, deciding she'd better get busy at something if she was going to stay on the farm . . . like finding a way to make a living. She'd had great intentions when she came back from Tulsa, but somehow the days had slipped by. The only thing she'd accomplished had been a trip to see Mr. Felker. He'd called yesterday to tell her he'd found someone to lease the chicken operation, but instead of making her feel better, it had made her feel worse. She decided she'd better start looking for a job today . . . really looking.

She was on her third cup of coffee when she heard the "Yoo-hoo" from the front yard. Gertie. As she opened the door, the aroma of fresh rolls met Melissa.

"Hadn't seen you in a few days, thought maybe you was over here wastin' away," the other woman said, smiling.

"Come in, Gertie. Whatever that is, it smells wonderful. We'll have coffee." Gertie followed her to the kitchen and unwrapped her pan. Thick, golden cinnamon rolls lay in gooey splendor in the pan. Melissa quickly fixed Gertie's coffee, then served each a roll. "These are incredible," she said around a bite.

"Well, I thought you might need a little cheerin' up and I think food always helps a body."

"These would cure anything." Melissa knew Gertie had more on her mind than food this morning. They ate in silence for a few moments.

"Melissa, I know it ain't none of my business, but that boy was by the house yesterday, and I ain't never seen anything quite so pitiful."

Melissa brightened. "Dave was there?"

"Yes, Davey. He came by to check our houses, see if they was ready for chicks. We been growin' chickens for him or his daddy for twenty years and he's never felt the need to check the houses till now." Gertie snorted and shook her head.

Melissa took a deep breath, wanting to know, yet not wanting to know. "Why was he there?"

"So he could stand in my backyard and stare at this place like a moonstruck calf, I reckon. He'd heard about Jasper Hanks leasin' this place, I guess. Old man Felker probably called him before he did you, probably told him Jasper leased the whole place. Anyhow, he's got an awful case of it. He knows he made a mess of things, but he's afraid to call you, afraid you're gone or won't talk to him. I sure would like to see you two patch it up."

"Oh, Gertie, so would I, but I don't know how." She felt tears sting her eyes. "I just don't know why he did it."

"Doubt if he does either. But his one fling at marriage stung him pretty good. She was a terrible woman to do what she did to him."

"What did she do?"

"Tried to make him into something he wasn't," Gertie said cryptically. "And that's all I'm gonna say on the subject, except I think you're both bein' awful proud and foolish about this thing."

Melissa finished her roll, but suddenly the taste was gone. Maybe he did still want her, but she just didn't know how to take back all those awful things she'd said. "I don't know Gertie. Maybe in a week or so..."

"Well, I told him he ought to just call you and get it straightened out. But he seems to be about as scared as you are. Well, I got to go. You think about it, honey."

Melissa watched Gertie walk down the road. It all sounded so easy when Gertie said it. She decided she would give him a week to call. If he hadn't called by then, she would...would what? She'd worry about that when the week was up. If he was as miserable as Gertie said, she could only wonder why he hadn't called.

CHAPTER TWELVE

DAVE FOLLOWED the white bus, just as he had eight weeks before, not seeing the fireball rising in the east, seeing only the dusty taillights of the bus ahead. He had gone in very early that morning, still pondering what to do, at the last minute deciding to go with the chicks—to go back to the farm and try to exorcise the ghosts that haunted his every waking moment.

As the bus turned into the driveway, he looked toward the house expecting her to come out on the porch, hair tousled and eyes full of sleep, but the house lay silent in the early dawn. He didn't even catch sight of Lady. He followed the bus up the hill, stalking into the first chicken house to see if things were ready. He noted with what satisfaction he could muster that the pans were full of feed and the waterers clean and ready, so unlike that other time. He shook himself like a wet dog, remembering that he was here to get rid of the ghosts.

He watched, a tall silent figure leaning against the wall, as the men dumped the baby chicks under the brooders. But every time he looked at the chicks, he saw Melissa as he had seen her the day his anger had turned to admiration and a little bit of love. He saw her bending over the bits of yellow fluff, talking to each as if it were the only one. He fled the chicken house, knowing the ghosts were getting worse, not better.

Driving down the hill, he noticed for the second time that Lady was nowhere in sight. He knew she would have taken the dog wherever she had gone. Melissa was not the type to take the dog to the pound, but it saddened him. He thought Lady would not be happy in Tulsa. She, like her mistress, belonged here. On an impulse, he stopped the truck. He had to take one last look at the house, seal it forever in his memory, maybe get rid of the picture of Melissa bent over the cardboard boxes, unwilling for even the least chick to die. It was that day he'd lost his heart.

Feeling like a trespasser, he decided to try the back door, assuming from the quietness of the house that the new occupants had not yet moved in. The silence seemed absolute, causing him to tiptoe up the steps. As his hand reached for the door handle, he peered through the dusty screen and froze. Time seemed to stand still as he stared at the scene in front of him. It was Melissa, silhouetted against the window and the morning sun, hair on fire with the light. She was standing over a cardboard box, a bit of yellow fluff nestled against her cheek.

Dave gasped and turned to lean against the house, rubbing his eyes. It looked so real. His mind raced. Maybe he was losing his mind, maybe he would never find peace. It couldn't be Melissa, she was gone. Even if it were Melissa, she couldn't have gotten any chicks, he would have seen her. He shook himself and moved back to the door, certain the apparition would be gone now, but as he opened the door, Melissa still stood there. "Melissa?" He felt stupid calling to a ghost, but the ghost turned to stare at him.

"Dave?" She stood, staring, hesitating, searching his face, then rushed to him with open arms. "Oh, Dave."

"Melissa?" He pulled her to him, relieved to feel her warm flesh. "I thought you were a ghost. Oh, Melissa, I thought I'd lost you." He showered her with kisses, touching her, reassuring himself.

Melissa seemed to melt in his arms, babbling about misunderstandings and forgiveness and other such nonsense. When they could regain their senses, Dave set her in a chair. "Honey, let's forget about all your explanations. I was the fool, not you. I just have to tell you why I was so stupid."

"It's not necessary, Dave."

"Yes, it is. I saw you at the auction. Then when you bought this place, I couldn't believe it. I couldn't get you out of my mind and that made me mad. Then when I saw you with those chicks, it got worse." He stroked her cheek. "The afternoon I walked in here and saw all those boxes of chicks, I lost my heart, Melissa. I've been in love with you since that day."

"Why didn't you say something?"

He shook his head. "I knew you were struggling to become your own woman. I guess I knew that the first day in my office. I don't know how I knew, but that was when the lie started. Then I fell hopelessly in love with you and I didn't know how to tell you. I guess I thought that one day it wouldn't matter."

"Oh, Dave. How could we both have been so dumb?"

He smiled and kissed her. "Good question. Let's just start all over again from this minute. I want to marry you. Now. As soon as possible, before you get away again."

Melissa smiled and reached up to kiss his cheek. She wanted to be sure this was not a dream. But her lips touched a real, warm, breathing cheek. His familiar scent was the last reassurance she needed. "You'll never get rid of me now. I love you, Dave." She smiled and leaned back in her chair, as assured and confident as if he'd never been away. "However, I think we should elope."

"Elope? You deserve better than that. I want to show you off to this whole town."

She chewed on her lower lip. "Well, you see, my mother has been planning my wedding since I was born. And according to her plan, one can't possibly get everything ready in less than four months. So, if I call her today, let's see, it would be...probably Christmas. There are the invitations, then all the showers, and of course..."

"I surrender. Forget it. We'll elope." He turned to the box on the floor where a chick was voicing its protest about something, then turned a stern face to Melissa. "I also want an explanation. What are you doing with chicks? You almost caused me cardiac arrest. I looked in here and thought I was seeing a ghost. Where did they come from?"

Melissa swelled up with pride. "Actually, it's a long story. Sure you want to hear it?"

"I'm sure. Anything that almost caused my premature demise deserves an explanation." He squeezed her hand, then turned it to kiss her soft palm.

Melissa shivered, but forced herself to ignore the gesture. After all, she didn't want him to think she'd been pining away for him. "Well, Gertie and Homer got chicks day before yesterday. If you kept track of your growers," she said smugly, "you'd know that." She ducked a swat and continued. "Well, I'd gotten used to chickens. I couldn't just get rid of them cold turkey, so to speak."

Dave groaned at the pun and covered his face. "Melissa, where did you get the chickens?"

She leaned close and whispered. "Gertie and I have conspired against Homer to rescue the sick ones. Gertie smuggles them over here in her bread basket."

Dave stared at her for a moment, then his laughter filled the kitchen. He pulled Melissa onto his lap and kissed her soundly. "I have missed you, woman. Don't ever change. If there's one thing I can provide you with on an unlimited basis, it's chickens. But we might have to try someplace besides the kitchen to take care of them."

"Oh, Dave, we can live here, can't we?"

He laughed again. Somehow he couldn't see catsup boxes full of chicks on Alicia's white carpet. "I'd love it. When you see the barn I live in, you'll know why I almost panicked the night you called and wanted to come over. We can live wherever you want to, sweetheart. By the way, where's Lady?"

"Off on her morning bunny hunt." She nibbled at his ear. "I'm so glad you came back. I missed you."

"By the way, how come somebody else has the chicken contract now and you're still here? That's another thing that almost gave me heart failure."

Melissa quickly explained all that had transpired, wondering the whole time how they could possibly have had a disagreement about anything. She nestled into his chest, happy again, feeling at home.

Dave found her mouth and his kiss was strong and deep. "Melissa . . ."

"Mmm . . . I'd love to, but Gertie is due any minute with another basket of chickens."

Dave held her and laughed, content with this wonderful woman who could give him so much love and still have so much left for God's least little creatures. He was still chuckling, watching Melissa hurry to straighten her clothes as the front door opened and a very loud, very conspiratorial whisper shattered the morning calm.

"Melissa? Lord, I got two baskets full this time."

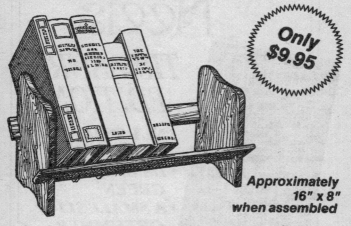

Here's how to get this special offer from Harlequin!

As simple as 1...2...3!

1. **Each month, save one Treasury Edition coupon from your favorite Romance or Presents novel.**
2. **In four months you'll have saved four Treasury Edition coupons (only one coupon per month allowed).**
3. **Then all you have to do is fill out and return the order form provided, along with the four Treasury Edition coupons required and $2.95 for postage and handling.**

Mail to: Harlequin Reader Service

In the U.S.A.
901 Fuhrmann Blvd.
P.O. Box 1397
Buffalo, NY 14240

In Canada
P.O. Box 609
Fort Erie, Ontario
L2A 9Z9

BN-Nov-2

Please send me my Special copy of the Betty Neels Treasury Edition. I have enclosed the four Treasury Edition coupons required and $2.95 for postage and handling along with this order form. (Please Print)

NAME_____

ADDRESS_____

CITY_____

STATE/PROV._____ ZIP/POSTAL CODE_____

SIGNATURE_____
This offer is limited to one order per household.

This special Betty Neels offer expires
February 28, 1987.

SUPPLIES LIMITED

Take 4 novels and a surprise gift FREE

Janet Dailey
Americana

Don't miss a single title from this great collection. The first eight titles have already been published. Complete and mail this coupon today to order books you may have missed.

Harlequin Reader Service

In U.S.A.
901 Fuhrmann Blvd.
P.O. Box 1397
Buffalo, N.Y. 14140

In Canada
P.O. Box 2800
Postal Station A
5170 Yonge Street
Willowdale, Ont. M2N 6J3

Please send me the following titles from the Janet Dailey Americana Collection. I am enclosing a check or money order for $2.75 for each book ordered, plus 75¢ for postage and handling.

————	ALABAMA	Dangerous Masquerade
————	ALASKA	Northern Magic
————	ARIZONA	Sonora Sundown
————	ARKANSAS	Valley of the Vapours
————	CALIFORNIA	Fire and Ice
————	COLORADO	After the Storm
————	CONNECTICUT	Difficult Decision
————	DELAWARE	The Matchmakers

Number of titles checked @ $2.75 each = $_____

N.Y. RESIDENTS ADD
  APPROPRIATE SALES TAX $_____

Postage and Handling $___.75___

                TOTAL $_____

I enclose _____

(Please send check or money order. We cannot be responsible for cash sent through the mail.)

PLEASE PRINT

NAME _____

ADDRESS _____

CITY _____

STATE/PROV. _____